"You're gett... Jeffrey."

Cyd took his hand and squeezed. "I know just the antidote." The moment she'd been waiting for. The chance to take his mind off business.

Jeffrey pulled his hand from hers and started pacing. "You don't understand. This could make my career."

While he walked away from her, she quickly doffed her robe. And when he turned around... Honestly, she'd never seen a man stare at her like that. His eyes were shiny, focused right on her.

She placed her hands behind her head, the way she'd seen a pinup poster girl do. For extra effect, Cyd thrust out one hip.

Jeffrey's hot gaze traveled along her arms, down to that thrust-out hip, then back.

"What are you doing?" he said in a choked voice.

"Taking a hot bath. You should, too. It's the perfect way to relax," she answered, trying to sound coy and suggestive. She swiveled ever so slowly and walked toward the tub, hoping that he'd follow her.

And the squeak in the floorboard told her he was doing just that.

Dear Reader,

Too Close for Comfort and its sequel, *Too Close To Call*, Temptation #940 by Barbara Dunlop, are the result of a brainstorming session where Barbara and I gleefully latched on to the idea of a *"Parent Trap* for adults" story. Two guys from totally different backgrounds— one's a rugged Alaskan, the other a sophisticated big-city executive—discover they're twins and, as a last-stop ploy to ensure the success of a major business venture, swap places.

In my book, Jeffrey Bradshaw, senior executive for Argonaut Studios in Los Angeles, takes a trip to a remote region of Alaska to research the location for a TV series…and gets stuck there! Think James Bond stuck in Fargo. No martinis, no five-star hotels… But Jeffrey's greatest challenge is matching wits with a feisty, wild-hearted bush pilot named Cyd Thompson who's more woman than Jeffrey has ever handled. Hey, when it gets too close for comfort, maybe the best thing to do is just get closer….

To read about my upcoming books, as well as enter contest for prizes, please visit my Web site at http://www.colleencollins.net.

Happy reading,

Colleen Collins

Books by Colleen Collins

TOO CLOSE FOR COMFORT
Colleen Collins

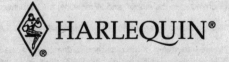

HARLEQUIN®

TORONTO • NEW YORK • LONDON
AMSTERDAM • PARIS • SYDNEY • HAMBURG
STOCKHOLM • ATHENS • TOKYO • MILAN • MADRID
PRAGUE • WARSAW • BUDAPEST • AUCKLAND

To Barbara Dunlop,
who made brainstorming this series too much fun!

Acknowledgments: Special thank-yous to Jay Kelley,
Fly Alaska, who walked (flew?) me through the world of being a
bush pilot in Alaska; Sara "the Stove Princess" at the Good Time
Stove Company for educating me about oil stoves; Matt Carolan for
letting me pick his brain about life in the Alaskan interior;
and Shaun for the writing cheers during deadline.

ISBN 0-373-69139-4

TOO CLOSE FOR COMFORT

This edition published by arrangement with Harlequin Books S.A.

® and TM are trademarks of the publisher. Trademarks indicated with ® are registered in the United States Patent and Trademark Office, the Canadian Trade Marks Office and in other countries.

Visit us at www.eHarlequin.com

Printed in U.S.A.

1

JEFFREY BRADSHAW STEPPED FROM the mind-numbing outdoors into the heated reception area, glad his breaths no longer emitted clouds of vapor. He flicked his wrist and checked his Rolex. Almost 4:00 p.m. He looked up. No monitors to announce if his four o'clock flight was on time. And if he glanced out the window outside, no commuter planes on the tarmac. Jeffrey looked around at the Alpine "Airport," which consisted of a pop machine, an assortment of chairs and a counter. He headed toward the latter, pounding his hands together and wishing to hell it would stun the blood to start pumping again. So this was autumn in Alaska. Frozen land. Frigid air. *What I'd give for a hot tub, a hot toddy and a very, very hot woman.*

"Can I help you?" The guy behind the counter was fiddling with his computer.

"True North Airlines?"

The fellow did a funny salute. "You got it. I'm Wally."

Jeffrey smiled while trying not to stare at Wally's blazing red plaid shirt. Maybe all Alaskans wore such shirts in case they got stuck in a snowstorm. "Flight to Arctic Luck," Jeffrey said. "Four p.m." He reached into the inner pocket of his Italian cashmere suit jacket, pulled out his wallet and extracted a credit card. "One. Jeffrey Bradshaw."

Wally took the credit card, giving Jeffrey an odd look. In certain circles, Jeffrey was accustomed to people recognizing him. At thirty-four, he'd held prominent executive positions at several global corporations, the most recent being Acquisitions Director at Argonaut Studios in Los Angeles. Just last month *Forbes* had done an article on how Jeffrey increased Argonaut's profits in the third quarter by a phenomenal fifteen percent due to his innovative business ideas. The article even made Jeffrey look like a damn movie star by plastering a photo of him and a hot new television actor, Gordon Tork, on the cover.

Not bad for a kid who grew up on the streets. But growing up tough had been a bonus for Jeffrey. He had both street savvy and business savvy, which meant he could deal with just about any type of personality thrown at him, from cons to CEOs.

And this Wally fell somewhere in-between. A decent guy, probably born and raised in Alaska. So it would surprise Jeffrey if Wally, working at a one-person airport counter in remote Alpine, Alaska, had seen the *Forbes* article and recognized Jeffrey.

As the card cleared, Wally continued staring at Jeffrey, then glanced behind his shoulder, then back to Jeffrey.

Jeffrey looked over Wally's shoulder into a square mirror where he caught his reflection. Strange. His neatly trimmed dark brown hair curled over his collar in the mirror. That's when he realized it was no mirror, but a *window*. And he was staring into some guy's face who was looking back at him, his hazel eyes flashing surprise.

It was like looking into some kind of distorted reflection, as though Jeffrey were seeing a more craggy, weathered version of himself.

Hell, it *was* like looking at himself. There was that damn cowlick he'd wrestled with his entire life, right at the crown of his—well, that guy's—head. Even the size of his—well, that guy's, too—ears. Jeffrey never thought his ears were *that* big, but several girlfriends had giggled they were the biggest, sexiest ears they'd ever whispered into.

Jeffrey squinted.

Yeah, that guy definitely had his ears.

What were the odds that two men, in a chance encounter, looked alike, had matching cowlicks and the same big, sexy ears? Had to be less than one percent of the population of the entire world. No, even less than that.

I'm losing it.

He wiped his hand across his face, welcoming the cold jolt of snow crystals that still clung to his leather glove. Seeing transmutations of himself had to be the effects of the long flight from New York to Anchorage, then the commuter hop here to Alpine. Throw in some stale airline peanuts, and anyone would see things.

Outside, the roar of an engine distracted him. His gaze shifted to another window, through which he saw a Cessna barreling at some insane angle toward the ground. Jeffrey was always aware of the impression he was making, but nothing could have stopped him from yelling an expletive and pointing toward the impending crash.

"Looks like Thompson's right on time," said Wally.

Stunned, Jeffrey watched as the plane jerked up at the last moment, its wheels miraculously touching the tarmac before the machine shuddered to a stop with mere feet of asphalt to spare.

Jeffrey waited until his pounding heart leveled off. "Is Thompson the pilot flying to Arctic Luck?"

"You bet."

"I want another flight." No way in hell was he getting into some stunt pilot's death-wish plane.

"No other flights to Arctic Luck today."

"Is this an airport?"

Wally paused, his clear blue eyes taking in Jeffrey. "It is."

"Then call whoever's in charge. Get another flight here." Jeffrey hadn't graduated Princeton's business school summa cum laude, and been a successful business maverick, without learning a few tricks about managing people. He glanced at a handwritten sign taped onto Wally's computer. Keep The Customer Satisfied. "Because I'm a customer and I want satisfaction."

Wally tapped a key on the computer, then shifted his weight so he faced Jeffrey. "We'd be more than happy, Mr. Bradshaw, to get you another flight, but our most recent weather bulletin says there's a storm building off the Gulf. Thompson's our best bush pilot and, right now, your only option for a flight to Arctic Luck."

On cue, a wiry teenage boy dressed in jeans and a parka pushed open the swinging door from the hangar. Pausing, he shoved back his baseball cap and raked fingers through his short, black hair. Upon seeing Jeffrey, his big brown eyes widened, then swerved to look at the guy in the window.

Wally waved a paper at the boy, who did another doubletake at Jeffrey and the guy in the window before accepting the paper. He promptly looked at it, then back at Jeffrey with a broad grin. "Howdy."

The voice was...softer than Jeffrey expected. "Hello."

The kid held out his hand.

Jeffrey paused, then offered his. For such a small hand, this teenager sure had a hearty shake. "You're Thompson?"

"Yes. You're heading to Arctic Luck?"

Was this kid even old enough for a pilot's license? Wonderful. An illegal, daredevil pilot. Jeffrey learned long ago to never accept "no" for an answer. Keep stalling, asking for another flight to Arctic Luck, and things could happen. "I'm taking another flight."

The boy released the handshake. "Then you're going to be waiting for a long time." He held up the paper. "Storm's coming in."

"So I've heard."

The boy grinned again, then swaggered off to the pop machine. But instead of inserting coins, he gave it a calculated punch that released a drink.

"Are you canceling or taking the flight?" asked Wally.

Jeffrey weighed his odds. He could forego this trip to Arctic Luck, which meant he wouldn't have the first-hand data he needed at the Argonaut board meeting early Monday morning. A key meeting where Harold Gauthier, chairman of the board, was making a special appearance to hear the pros and cons for the Alaskan film series Jeffrey was pitching, a romantic comedy along the lines of *Ed* meets *Northern Exposure* to be called *Sixty Below*. Not only was Jeffrey overseeing this deal, he'd written the story, which he'd set in a hypothetical Alaskan town. But now that the deal was nearing closure, it was imperative Jeffrey actually *see* the proposed location so he could speak formidably about how this frontier town was integral to the success of the series.

He had originally planned on flying in today, Saturday, then researching Arctic Luck tonight and tomorrow. Later on Sunday, he'd scheduled flights back to Alpine, then Anchorage, with a final flight to Los Angeles late Sunday night. He'd then catch some shut-eye and be ready for Monday morning's meeting.

His alternative plan? To not fly to Artic Luck because he had a ten percent chance of dying thanks to Thompson's death-defying flying tactics.

And then there was the issue of his promotion from acquisitions director to vice president of development at Argonaut Studios. Cinching this series would cinch the title.

"Yes, I still want to take the flight." Jeffrey took in a sobering breath of air and hoped it wasn't his last.

CYD THOMPSON WAITED at the door to the hangar for Mr. Big City to hustle over his smug self so she could usher him to the plane. As he sauntered toward her, she checked him out. Pretty fancy clothes, there. Fancy and damn impractical. Hadn't anybody warned him that those leather loafers wouldn't prevent his feet from freezing if the snow was sticking to the ground in Arctic Luck? And that coat—it would keep him warm for, oh, maybe three seconds. Give or take a second.

She stared at his face. Eerie how he looked like her boss, Jordan, who owned True North Airlines. Cyd rarely got unnerved, but seeing the resemblance had definitely thrown her off.

She glanced at the window to Jordan's office. Damn amazing how these two guys shared the same hair— rich molasses color with that funky wave at the crown. And although Mr. City Slicker had barely smiled a greeting, something about his and Jordan's smiles were alike, too. The way their lips crooked a little to the side, kinda like Harrison Ford.

"Ready?" Mr. City Slicker, tucking his wallet neatly into the inside of his jacket, looked questioningly at her.

Jeez, even their voices were similar. Rock-bottom husky. Although Mr. City Slicker definitely had more of an edge to his. But then, most city people did.

"Yes, but you aren't."

He paused, his hazel eyes flashing her a look she couldn't decipher. "I'm ready," he responded, that edge in his voice sharpening.

Didn't anybody ever disagree with this guy? Or

did he carry a permanent chip on that fancy jacket shoulder?

Or maybe she was being too brusque. Jordan had coached her about this, over and over, asking her to please be less rough around the edges. In all her twenty-five years, nobody had ever told her to be "less rough" as though she were some kind of lump of coal with the remote potential to be a diamond.

But Jordan seemed hell-bound to polish her, give her etiquette lessons, all the while saying she wasn't to take it personally. "It's not about you," he'd remind her. "It's about the customer. Remember, the customer is king."

And making the customer king meant more business for True North Airlines.

"I, uh, meant do you have everything you need?" She plastered on one of those syrupy-sweet smiles like those cover girl types on magazines.

Mr. Big City did a double take, then frowned a little. "My luggage is on its way to L.A., so I'm carrying everything I need."

L.A. Figured. "I didn't catch your name," she said, forcing herself to sound polite, interested. Man, this customer relations stuff was exhausting. Good thing this was a short flight.

"Jeffrey."

She waited for more.

"Bradshaw."

This conversation made small talk seem downright itsy-bitsy. "And you're from L.A.?"

He gave her another of those indecipherable looks. "No, New York. For the past year, anyway."

"Going back to live in L.A.?"

"Do you always ask so many questions?"

Only while Jordan is on this customer relations kick. "Only when I'm interested." *Or sort of interested.* Besides, if she got employee of the month, that little bonus check would come in real handy.

"Yes, I'm going back to L.A. I'm in Alaska checking out a location for a potential television series."

"In Arctic Luck?" she blurted.

He nodded.

Shock raced through her. She'd spent years of her life loving this pristine wilderness, especially her hometown of Arctic Luck. No way some big-city business was going to destroy the land she called home, be that Arctic Luck or anywhere in Alaska for that matter. Especially the kind of business that had destroyed her father.

To hell with customer relations. Screw the bonus. She glared at the city slicker. "Follow me," she snapped, opening the hangar door. "The plane's ready."

As they headed toward the Cessna, she paused next to a wheeled rack that normally held passengers' luggage. Considering this was the time of year when fierce snowstorms started moving in, with tourism dropping more dramatically than the temperatures, these carts were used for things other than luggage—such as food, supplies, propane—things that bush planes flew to remote, snow-locked communities.

She grabbed a parka off the rack and tossed it to the guy. "Put this on."

He caught the heavy parka with one hand, not looking strained at all. Cyd fought the urge to be impressed.

"I don't need this," he said matter-of-factly.

"Fine with me if you want to freeze off your tush."

He cocked one eyebrow.

"If you think it's cold on the ground, just wait till we're at a thousand feet. Men have been known to get frostbite on their nose, ears and—"

"I'll wear it." He set down his carry-on and began unbuttoning his coat.

With a shake of her head, Cyd kept walking to the plane. Wouldn't that be her luck, to be carting some city jerk to her hometown. She shouldn't help him anymore. Not an iota. Because every time she did, she was aiding and abetting the enemy.

"Just hurry up," she snapped, putting a bit more "rough around the edges" in her voice than usual. "I have a run to Eagle Nest after Arctic Luck and the weather's kicking up."

But another plan was already forming in Cyd's mind.

THE WEATHER KICKING UP? Ten minutes later, Jeffrey thought his heart was kicking up, and *out* of his body. From what he could see outside the cockpit window, snowflakes were thickening, swirling in the wind. It was like flying through a messy potato soup. A very, very cold potato soup. He tried to stop looking at the temperature gauge, but he had a head for numbers. And thirty below zero was a mind-numbing number.

"Cold?" asked Thompson.

"You b-bet my tush." Damn if his teeth weren't chattering. Even with this fur-lined, Paul-Bunyon-size parka on.

The plane lurched again.

"Weather sucks," said Thompson, "but even if we're forced down, it would be a smooth crash landing because of the flat terrain, Johnny—"

"Jeffrey." If he was going to die, he wanted to be called by his right name.

"Lousy visibility," Thompson muttered, tapping one of the gauges with a finger. He shot a look at Jeffrey. "Don't worry. Sometimes the instruments freeze up a bit, but I can still manage. This is a piece of cake."

He hated cake. Hated this plane. Hated potato soup.

Thompson muttered something else under his breath. It sounded like "damn snow squall" and Jeffrey wished he wasn't so attuned to words. From an early age, his greatest escape was reading novels and listening to music. Being bumped from foster home to foster home, how often had he escaped feeling like the outsider by cracking open a book or slapping on a pair of headphones? With music, the heavier the lyrics, the better.

His love of words had extended to his business life as well. While others analyzed body language, he analyzed the tone of people's voices, how they used words, and eighty percent of the time, he had a person pegged.

But at this moment, he hated words. Especially ones like "damn snow squall" and "lousy visibility." Thompson had an attitude three times his body size. And although Jeffrey had had his fair share of threats in his life, he'd never been threatened by a pilot, for God's sake. That's how it felt, anyway, with Thompson's insinuations about a potential crash landing.

Jeffrey shifted in his seat, wondering if his jaw would ever unclench. And wishing to hell he had something to distract him. "Got any music?" he asked tightly.

Thompson nodded and flicked a switch. A throbbing bass filled the cockpit, followed by Bruce Springsteen's gravelly voice, wailing about tramps and being born to run. Jeffrey shot Thompson a look. Was this kid crazy, playing a searing rock tune at a time like this? Jeffrey eased out a stream of air. *Well, if now's my time to die, might as well be with The Boss.*

"Katimuk area traffic, this is Cessna 4747sierra." Thompson spoke loudly, clearly into the headset mouthpiece while checking the GPS on the dashboard.

Katimuk? Jeffrey frowned. *Must be a town near Arctic Luck.*

"Nine miles west of Katimuk over the river. Eastbound for Katimuk landing strip. Visibility limited. Flying at one thousand."

Katimuk landing strip. Maybe Arctic Luck shared the same landing area. Or maybe weather was forcing them down. *God, wish I hadn't had that last thought. Shoot me now.* Jeffrey leaned his head back against the headrest, grateful for something solid.

The plane plunged.

Jeffrey's stomach plummeted.

Springsteen wailed about sex.

Danger, death and sex had never been Jeffrey's calling card, but suddenly he was living it, moment by moment. Maybe he should have done the predictable things in life. Like gotten married, had children. Then he'd have heirs to his New York loft, L.A. condo, cars, stocks, investments. But when the women's faces whom he dated flashed through his mind, it was a blur of greedy eyes and sculpted cheeks. A montage of arm-candy dates, the kind of feminine assets that enhanced a guy's business allure at social functions.

Not a one of them the type to bake cookies, raise kids, grow old with.

For a fleeting moment, Jeffrey wondered if he'd made the right choices in life. He'd been so desperate to escape the streets, he'd worked hard to earn good grades, earn a college scholarship, land in a profession where he could make the big bucks.

But at this moment, maybe his last moment, he wondered what the big bucks really bought him. An expensive funeral?

"Katimuk traffic," continued Thompson, "Cessna 4747sierra is over the town entering a left downwind for landing to the west. Tell Harry to be there."

Harry? The thought flew from his mind as the plane careened. Jeffrey swore his internal organs swapped places as the aircraft dropped and dipped. In the background, Bruce rasped about some girl wrapping her legs around velvet rims.

Thompson was flicking switches, tugging the stick.

A clunking sound. The nose of the plane pitched up.

"Flaps," Thompson calmly explained, pulling on the yoke.

Jeffrey swallowed, hard. *Flaps. Good.*

Thompson reached for the ceiling and pulled something. "Trimming."

Trimming. Good. Whatever the hell that meant.

A runway appeared through a break in the fog. Jeffrey had never been so damn glad to see a strip of snowflaked dirt in his entire life. Something dark and bulky trotted across it. A moose?

Bruce was crooning about madness in his soul while Jeffrey prayed his last image on earth wouldn't be a close-up of a moose. Fortunately the beast jogged off the landing strip, disappearing into a white expanse of fog and snow.

The wheels hit solid ground.

Jeffrey released a pent-up breath, debating who ruled the world. Springsteen or Thompson.

And when the plane eased to a smooth stop, the answer was evident. *Thompson.*

"WE'RE WHERE?" Ten minutes ago, they'd landed. Jeffrey would have kissed the ground, but didn't want to end up with his lips frozen to it. He'd helped Thompson tie down the plane, then made the fatal mistake of asking where, exactly, they were.

"Katimuk."

That's what he thought Thompson had said the first time. Jeffrey chose his battles carefully, and had the common sense to not argue in body-freezing weather, but at the moment he had an issue to chew and didn't give a damn if his words froze midsentence.

"I need to go to Arctic Luck." Hell, he needed a lot more than that. A hot drink, for starters. His throat felt like he'd swallowed a block of ice.

"Good for you," yelled Thompson, marching away from him. "Say hello when you get there."

Where was Thompson going? Jeffrey jogged a few feet to catch up, tripping and sliding over icy patches. "I demand you take me to Arctic Luck," he yelled, his words escaping in plumes of vapor. "I *paid* to go to Arctic Luck."

Thompson stopped, turned, and fisted his hands on his slim hips. "I, I, I! You big-city types never think of others, only yourselves."

This conversation was taking a bigger turn than some of those insane plane maneuvers Thompson had made. Thompson, *definitely* no longer ruled the world. "My jacket is still on the plane. I need to get it."

"Where on the plane?"

Jeffrey blew out another gust of vapor. "I left it on the convenience luggage rack with my carry-on, to be loaded onto the plane."

"Convenience?" Thompson paused, then barked a laugh. "What'd you think? That some flight attendant would *conveniently* transport your stuff onto the plane? I don't think so."

"That jacket has my ID, my money—"

"Those fancy shoes of yours are gonna freeze to the

ground if we don't keep walking." Thompson turned and started marching away.

Jeffrey glanced down, but only briefly. Better to keep walking than staring at his feet which might become one with the earth at any moment. He kept up a brisk pace behind Thompson. In the dense fog, he swore he heard the barking of dogs.

"Yo, Harry, over here!" Thompson yelled.

Through the fog, Jeffrey spied a line of dogs—looked to be twelve, maybe fourteen—hitched to a sled.

A beefy guy dressed in a regulation parka waved. "Storm's on its way."

Thompson stopped next to what looked like some kind of basket seat on the sled. Harry stood on board runners behind the basket.

"Get in," Thompson ordered.

On closer inspection, the basket looked small. Too small for two people. "How do we do this?" asked Jeffrey.

Thompson made a sound somewhere between a grunt and a snort. "Now's not the time to analyze options, city boy. Just get in."

Harry laughed.

One of the dogs howled.

Jeffrey wished he were back in the plane. Suddenly it seemed far preferable to be risking death in the sky than death with a pack of dogs and two surly parka people. But as now wasn't the time to be analyzing options or death, he swung one leg, then the other, into the basket and sat down.

Thompson stepped one jean-clad leg inside, then slid into a sitting position on Jeffrey's lap. "Let's go!"

A whip cracked. The dog team lurched forward, suddenly silent and all business. Harry yelled commands.

Thompson shifted, pressing against Jeffrey.

Before now, he had been stunned by the cold. Then by Mr. Toad's wild plane ride. Followed by this adventure with a traveling dog team.

But nothing was as stunning as the feel of a curvy rump molded against his stomach and the undeniable roundness of a breast pressed against his cheek.

Thompson, he realized, was a woman.

2

THE DOG SLED PULLED UP in front of a rustic, oversize cabin and stopped. The lead Husky uttered a sharp whine of satisfaction and crouched low in the snow. Other team dogs started yelping and barking, some showing impatience with the restraint of the harnesses, some sniffing the air.

Amid the cacophony, the snow fell silently from a darkening sky in large, white flakes.

Cyd turned to Jeffrey. "Time to get out."

But time played a trick on her.

It stopped.

Or maybe it had stopped minutes ago, somewhere on the sled ride from the landing strip to this lodge while their bodies had been molded together in this one-person basket. Yes, it had stopped then, wrapping the world around them, creating a place where only the two of them existed.

That's when she'd tried not to notice how nicely his body conformed to hers. Tried not to admire his strength, or how his arm had wrapped around her, holding her close, as though protecting her.

Nobody, especially no *man*, needed to protect Cyd Thompson.

But she hadn't budged from Jeffrey's embrace.

And, if she were perfectly honest with herself, she still didn't want to budge. Which irked her as much as excited her. Maybe it was because she was accustomed to fighting the elements and competing with the guys. Add to that her role as head of the household since her dad died, and Cyd Thompson was a one-woman force who bowed to no one.

But at this precarious moment, Cyd felt all those attributes turning on her. Sharing that tight space with Jeffrey, she'd felt his power, sensed his manliness. And dammit all to hell, the experience left her feeling...*womanly.*

He's a city slicker, she reminded herself. *Out to destroy your world.*

She turned and boldly met Jeffrey's gaze, ready to say something "rough around the edges."

But she got lost in his eyes.

They looked like Jordan's. A deep reddish brown, intelligent. But Jordan's eyes didn't flash with specks of green and gold. And Jordan sure didn't look back at her the way Jeffrey did, with a mixture of surprise and interest.

Interest?

She shifted in the basket, too aware of his solid thigh muscle molded against her hip. A city boy with muscles? Her mind reeled with how he came by those...and worse, her imagination joined the free-for-all and flashed an image of what he probably looked like naked. All muscle and sinew and dark, curly hair...

City Boy. Big business. End of the world.

"I said it's time to go!" she barked, grabbing the edge of the basket and blowing out a gust of air as though that would also blow out these crazy thoughts.

But she made a serious mistake when she paused and glanced into Jeffrey's face again.

He still had that look of interest, but this time she also saw...amusement?

"What's so funny?" she snapped.

He blinked in exaggeration. "Just wondered why you're taking your time."

"It's cold."

"But you *live* in Alaska. You're used to it."

He had a point. But before she could muster some sassy response, he spoke again.

"But I don't mind if you want to stay wrapped around my body. I like it. It's keeping me warm." He grinned. A sexy, "gotcha" grin that did funny things to her insides.

Had to be the basket. Throwing two bodies into a space that was supposed to only hold one had messed up their equilibrium. Had created a world where body heat got mistaken for something more.

And that look in Jeffrey's eyes told her he felt that "something more," too. Time to get her footing back, literally. Time to take control, let him know who's boss.

"Time to get out," she said, or meant to say. Her words had escaped on a breathy stream of air. And she may have forgotten to say the last two words. Which meant she'd just whispered a suggestive, "Time to..." to this hunk of big-city hot love.

Heat surged to her cheeks.

Jeffrey's eyes did a slow perusal of her face, taking it all in. Then he nodded. A slow, knowing nod. Damn the man. Not breaking eye contact, either. As though willing her, no *defying* her, to admit that this sizzling, out-of-control moment was happening.

Well, she'd break this crazy moment, *now*.

Maneuvering herself to get out, her cheek brushed against Jeffrey's. *Ooooo.* He smelled deliciously spicy and musky. No northern guy smelled like *that*.

Stop smelling, keep moving.

She hoisted herself up to a crouched position. *When the hell is he going to break eye contact?* It was a matter of pride, but she wanted him to be the first. *Had* to be the first.

"Problem?" Jeffrey asked, his voice spicier than that damn cologne he wore.

She was hunched over, her butt in the air, her feet still in the basket. "You always stare like that?"

"Like what?"

"You know what I mean."

"Well, you're staring at me, too, you know." He winked.

With a huff of indignation, and anger because *she* was breaking the all-important stare-down, Cyd hurled herself out of the basket and landed with a splash in a hole of snow and slush.

She turned, her hands fisted on her hips, waiting to see how Mr. City Slicker landed on the icy snow with those plushy leather shoes. She just prayed he hit a hole big enough to sink him knee-deep in wet snow. What a shame, it would mess up those fancy slacks, too.

Jeffrey, *still* staring at her, cocked an eyebrow as though reading her mind and accepting the challenge. He stood—giving her an eyeful of his six-foot-plus being—swung one leg, then the other, over the side of the basket. He landed in slush, without the messy splash she'd made, and stepped neatly onto a path of crusty snow.

"You're gonna need boots," she said sharply, turning and trudging toward the door of the Mush Lodge.

"Wait," called out Jeffrey.

She barely turned, her feet still walking. "What?"

"I have a problem."

About time he admitted it. Feeling more in control, she turned. "What is it?"

He stopped, his feet spread apart, a lazy grin creasing his lips. "Don't know your name."

"Thompson."

"I know that one. Do you have a first name, or do you go by one name only. Like Cher and Madonna do."

Cher? Madonna? She glared at him. "Cyd Thompson."

He bowed a little, and damn if he didn't look like the ultimate gentleman paying his respects. The snow fell on his dark hair, sprinkling him with a little Alaskan magic. "Nice to meet you, Cyd Thompson."

Harry strolled past, letting roll a loud guffaw as he tucked away his mobile radiophone. "You two gonna keep playin' Romeo and Juliet in the snow, or come inside where it's warm?"

Juliet? Whatever had happened in the basket, Cyd wanted to leave it there. Jeffrey Bradshaw was bad news. Plus, now that Harry had seen that little bowing number, she'd never hear the end of it.

But worse was Jeffrey's reason for being here. He wanted to bring a frigging television series to her beloved Alaska, and Cyd reminded herself that she had to do whatever it took to stop him and his big-business, people-destroying machine. It destroyed her dad, and no way in hell would she let it destroy her family, her world.

"No more bowing," she muttered in Jeffrey's direction, avoiding his eyes.

Jeffrey grinned as Cyd spun on her heel and began marching toward the lodge. So he'd gotten to her, *again. Chalk that up as a point against me.*

Jeffrey followed her, their chilly silence broken by the crunch of the snow and the barking dogs. He let his gaze slide down her parka to that cute little jean-clad behind that bounced provocatively as she marched along. He liked her size—small and compact—and he had to admit, he liked her attitude, too. Reminded him of the tough girls he'd known growing up. The kind you could let down your guard with, smoke a cig, see the world for what it really was.

He hadn't known a woman like that in years.

No, since then, the women he'd known were at the opposite end of the spectrum. And they all had temperaments that ranged from a little rainfall to a little sunshine.

Cyd, on the other hand, was an entire weather system unto herself. A raging snowstorm one moment—and if he pegged her right in that hot little moment back in the sled—a sizzling heat wave the next.

She took the steps two at a time onto the porch, then swung open a heavy wooden door over which hung a sign that read Mush Lodge.

Jeffrey barely caught the door before she let it slam shut behind her.

As he stepped inside the golden-hazed interior of what appeared to be a cabin-turned-tavern, he guessed that Weather Cyd was at the moment a tornado. Hellbent to blast her way to what she wanted, and best of luck to Jeffrey if he got in her path.

He had no idea what irked her so much about him, but he had one hundred percent confidence in his charm factor. He'd get her to warm up.

Pulling the door shut behind him, he inhaled the scents. Coffee. Grilled meat and onions. The sounds of laughter and talking competed with background music—an old Neil Young tune about a cinnamon girl. Several big dogs slept in front of a large crackling fire to his right. A line of burly guys, with more hair than Jeffrey had seen since the rerelease of the movie *Woodstock*, lined the bar, swigging beer.

In the corner of the bar was a teenage boy, reading a book. A memory flashed through Jeffrey's mind. He'd been sixteen, living with a foster family in Philadelphia. A local bartender had befriended him, letting him visit whenever Jeffrey needed an escape. He'd been underage, but nobody questioned his being there because he kept to himself, minded his own business. He'd spent hours in that bar, reading authors like Bradbury and Kerouac who helped him escape his world.

Something clunked at his feet.

Cyd stood before him, a gleam in her dark chocolate eyes. "Put those on."

He looked down. A pair of scuffed, whiskey-colored boots lay on the floor. He looked back up into those chocolate eyes. She didn't fool him for a millisecond with that brusque attitude. This lady might be tough on the outside, but he'd seen beyond her exterior back at the sled. Inside, Cyd was soft and vulnerable.

Or maybe he understood that about her because once upon a time he'd known what it felt like to wear a chip on your shoulder and an ache in your heart.

"Thanks." He picked up the boots by their thick laces.

"Put them on while I radio Jordan back at Alpine. Need to file my report and tell him we didn't make Arctic Luck, and we're weathered in here." She started walking away across the rough-hewn floor, ignoring one of the guy's calling out "Hey, Juliet!" while another added, "Somebody protect the mirror and chairs!" Both comments were followed by raucous laughter.

"Wait."

Cyd turned.

"What do you mean, we're 'weathered in'?"

A corner of her pert mouth turned upward. "I mean we ain't goin' nowhere soon." She turned and continued walking.

With a shake of his head, Jeffrey followed. He had twenty-four hours to do research in Arctic Luck, not Kati-whatever.

He followed her into a small room that housed some bookshelves, a hot plate and a radio on a thick wooden table. The scent of coffee lingered in the air. Cyd was sitting on a metal folding chair at the table and fiddling dials on the radio.

"Operator, this is Mush Lodge calling YJ17546, True North Airlines on the Alpine Channel," she said into the mike.

This woman impressed him at the damnedest moments. Just when she'd irritated him to the point of his wanting to throttle her, she took life by the reins in an admirable display of focus and determination. When other women stomped away, he usually found them pouting in some corner. Not Cyd. If she ended up in a corner, she'd be figuring out how to fight her way back out.

"This is Alpine YJ17546," answered a man's voice through the radio static.

"Hey, Jordan, Cyd here."

"Everything okay?"

"It's fine. Had to land in Katimuk due to the storm."

"Roger, that. I'll change your flight plan. You get lost?"

"Uh, not really."

"How'd you end up in Katimuk?"

"Uh, yeah. I guess I did lose a few landmarks."

Jeffrey felt his antennae waving. He'd heard the truth in her voice. *She could have landed in Arctic Luck, but flew here instead.*

"Who're you talking to?" Jeffrey demanded.

She glanced over her shoulder, shooting him a "don't butt in" look.

Which had the opposite effect on Jeffrey. Nobody told him what *not* to do. He crossed the room in two strides and picked up the microphone. "Who is this?"

"Jordan Adamson, True North Airlines," a man responded. "Who's this?"

"Jeffrey Bradshaw. This is a disaster. I'm the passenger who paid to be flown to Arctic Luck, but I was flown to Kati-Kati—"

"Katimuk," said Cyd sweetly.

Jeffrey shot her a look.

There was a pause. "Sorry about that," said Jordan. "Can't fight the weather. But we'll get you to Arctic Luck as soon as possible."

"I need to get there *immediately*."

"Afraid we can't do that," said Jordan.

"That's impossible," said Cyd at the same time.

"Nothing's impossible," said Jeffrey. "I'll contact my office, have them call another airline."

"You can call," answered Jordan, "but nobody's going to fly in this."

"Why?" asked Jeffrey, eyeing Cyd while still talking into the microphone.

Cyd started to speak, but let Jordan answer. "Weathered in is weathered in," he explained calmly. "Nobody will risk an aircraft, and I'm sure you don't want to risk your life. Stick with Cyd. She knows what she's doing. She'll get you out as soon as possible."

Jeffrey didn't buy into her "so sorry" look. She was up to something.

"Let me get this straight," said Jeffrey, sitting on the table and lifting the microphone to speak into it. "Your pilot could have landed me in Artic Luck, but she flew me to Katimuk instead?"

Cyd pursed her lips.

"She landed where she felt the plane and passengers would be safe," Jordan said.

"Bull." Jeffrey glared at Cyd. She'd pulled a fast one, although he was clueless as to why. He'd get Jordan to fix this.

"Again, I'm sorry for the inconvenience," said Jordan. "True North Airlines will be happy to offer you a free round-trip passage to any city in the interior after the weather clears."

"I only want to go to Artic Luck. When will the weather clear?"

"No way to predict that," Jordan answered calmly. "My best guess is two days minimum, possibly a week."

"Neither option is acceptable." Jeffrey maintained eye contact with Cyd, who looked back at him with big eyes filled with concern and innocence. What a little actress. "I have a critical meeting in Los Angeles Monday morning which I *must* attend. My career depends on it.

This 'weathered in' is not n...
expect you to come up with a...

There was a long silence in th...
the sounds of laughter and music...

Jeffrey was accustomed to such...
ness. Person A created a problem and...
B to solve it. Jeffrey never accepted such...ssing
and always put the responsibility where i...y.

And at this moment, it lay with Jordan Adamson of
True North Airlines.

"I'll call you back in an hour," said Jeffrey, "to hear
how you're going to fix this situation." In New York or
L.A., an hour was always plenty of time to get someone's brain cells fired up with ideas.

"The situation will be the same in an hour," said Jordan. "You're right in the path of the storm front."

Now it was Jeffrey's turn to pause. Jordan, he had to
admit, was a worthy opponent. Cool-headed, in-
formed. He could use more managers like this back at
Argonaut. "Then I'll call you first thing in the morning,
at which time we'll discuss your solutions."

He handed the microphone back to Cyd, wondering
what the two of them would do for the rest of the night.

And wondering how to deal with this little dynamo
who seemed determined to screw up his plans.

CYD TOSSED BACK A WHISKEY, then slammed the shot
glass on the bar. She swiped her mouth with the back
of her hand, savoring the alcohol's stinging warmth as
it worked a path down her throat.

"Tough flight, Juliet?" asked Harry, his blue-green

...ing in a face that was all beard with room
...nose.

"You've known me for years, and suddenly you've
forgotten my name?" She motioned to Charlie, the
owner of the Mush Lodge, who was working the bar.

"Yep, known you for years, but never seen you have
so much trouble getting out of a damn sled...." Harry
let the sentence dangle as he took another sip of beer.

"Yeah?" Charlie said, wiping his hands on a towel.
Charlie had been in these parts as long as Cyd could remember. Some people said he'd landed here in the six-
ties in a psychedelic-painted school bus. Others said
he'd gone to Canada to avoid being drafted into the
Vietnam war, then relocated to this remote region of
Alaska when he met May, his wife.

He never explained his past. Or his future, for that
matter. He seemed pretty content to just live in the here
and now, tend the bar, play his favorite music. Grateful
Dead, Neil Young, the Stones.

"Coffee, don't be stingy with the cream," Cyd said.
"Please." She'd gotten so riled up over the last few
hours, she was losing her manners. Again. If she didn't
stay in practice, *try* to be polite, she'd get another of
those etiquette lessons from Jordan.

"Coffee, white. You got it, hon." Charlie nodded and
turned away.

"Jul-i-et," Harry sang under his breath before taking
another swig.

Cyd fought the urge to give him a piece of her mind.
She was one of the guys, dammit, not some girly Juliet.
One of the items on Jordan's customer relations cheat

sheet flashed through her mind. *Don't respond to criticism or taunts. Stay focused on the problem. Stay calm.*

She'd never thought about it before, but those rules were good for real life, too. She'd let Harry's comment go...but damn, it was hard trying to be good. If Jordan didn't want to win that Alaskan Tourism thing so bad, she'd blow off practicing being "polished" and just be her usual, feisty self.

Charlie set a steaming mug of coffee in front of her. "Hungry?"

"What're you grilling?"

"You," Harry chortled. Several of the guys laughed.

Cyd pursed her lips, determined to ignore him.

"Got some moose steak," answered Charlie, darting a glance at Harry, then back to Cyd.

"Get me some. Don't be stingy with the fries, either. And a salad." She almost forgot. "Please."

"Please?" Harry guffawed. "Where the hell you pick up *them* manners?"

That did it. Cyd swiveled on her bar stool and faced Harry. But just as she opened her mouth, Charlie cut in.

"Harry, May baked your favorite apple pie," said Charlie. "Wanna slice?"

Harry groaned like a bear. "May's apple pie? I've died and gone to heaven. Make that two slices."

"You got it." Charlie turned to go.

"Wait, Charlie," Cyd called out. "You seen Geraldine?" Geraldine, her aunt, lived on the outskirts of Katimuk.

"Yeah," Charlie answered over his shoulder.

"About two hours ago. She picked up supplies and headed back to her place."

Great. That meant Aunt Geri was home. Cyd wrapped her hands around the coffee mug, letting the warmth seep into her hands as she contemplated the carved names in the old oak bar top. Once upon a time, Harry had carved their names here, although both of them pretended to have forgotten.

The bar grew oddly silent.

She turned her head and looked down the stretch of worn oak.

Jeffrey stood at the end of the bar, looking like some kind of fancy thoroughbred surrounded by buffalo. He'd doffed his parka so everyone got an eyeful of his blue-and-white pin-striped, button-down shirt. She squinted. Were those *cuff links?*

"What'll you have?" asked Charlie. He'd paused halfway through the swinging kitchen door.

"Mind if I run a tab?"

"Brother, half of Katimuk does. What'll you have?"

"I could use a double martini, up, Bombay, twist."

"Bombay?" One of the guys snorted. "You got the wrong part of the world, buddy."

Everybody laughed. Somebody slapped the surface so hard, the entire bar rattled.

Charlie released the door and stepped back to the bar. Picking up a bottle of whiskey, he poured a shot and set it in front of Jeffrey. "Best I can do for a martini," he said, "unless you're a beer man."

"Thanks, this'll be great." Jeffrey downed it, then

glanced down the bar and made friendly, but direct, eye contact with each man.

Cyd released a pent-up breath. It appeared Jeffrey was up to the challenge and could handle this group.

"Anyone know where I can get a hotel room?" he asked.

On second thought, he couldn't.

As though a dam had burst, the entire group erupted in laughter and more table slapping.

"Yeah, there's a Hilton right down the road."

"Wait, let me call you a taxi."

"No, a limo!"

"Neither option is acceptable!" a guy yelled, evoking another explosion of laughter.

Jeffrey frowned in confusion. "Did you guys overhear?"

More laughter and bar thumping.

And Cyd thought the sled dogs made a hell of a racket.

Charlie returned from the kitchen, holding two plates of steaming apple pie in one hand. With the other, he poured more whiskey into Jeffrey's glass. "This one's on the house."

Jeffrey raised his drink. "To the great North." He tossed back the whiskey.

One by one, the guys raised their drinks, some muttering "to the North," some nodding solemnly. Cyd smiled. Mr. Jeffrey Bradshaw was showing that a thoroughbred could run with the pack. Damn if she wasn't more than a bit impressed. He might be all city slicker on the outside, but he almost seemed to have the soul of a Northerner. As though he knew what it was like to be fierce, independent, tough.

Jeffrey strolled down the bar and sat on the stool at the very end of the bar, next to Cyd.

Harry, sitting on the other side of Cyd, glanced over, but before he could say anything, Charlie plunked down the plates of pie in front of him. Harry inhaled as though he'd never sucked in a decent breath in his life, groaned something about May deserving sainthood, then dug in.

Relieved that Harry was distracted for the time being, Cyd turned to Jeffrey. She glanced down. "Got the boots on, I see."

He just looked at her, a twinkle in his eye. "Took me a while to figure them out."

She shot him a questioning look.

"I never have to lace up my Italian loafers."

She continued to stare at him, unblinking.

"I'm joking, Cyd."

She rolled back her shoulders. "I knew that." Her insides did a funny fluttering thing when Jeffrey flashed her that crooked, Harrison Ford-like smile.

Fortunately dinner arrived. The aroma of grilled meat and fries almost brought tears to Cyd's eyes. She hadn't eaten in hours, and it was all she could do to pick up a knife and fork and not dig into the meal with her bare hands.

"Looks good," Jeffrey commented. "What is it?"

"Mooth," she said with a full mouth.

Jeffrey gave her one of those quizzical looks, then nodded.

She swallowed. "Want some? Charlie makes killer homemade fries, too."

"Uh, I'll pass."

Jeffrey checked out the back of the bar, his eyes landing on a Crock-Pot. "Got some soup there?" he asked Charlie.

"Caribou stew."

Jeffrey paused. "Nothing with chicken or fish?" He didn't dare ask if they had a vegetarian plate. Not unless he wanted to be attacked by a horde of moosemen.

Charlie, rubbing a glass with a red-checkered cloth, shook his head.

"I'll take a bowl of that, then." He lifted his empty shot glass. "And hit me again." If he numbed himself enough, he wouldn't think about what he was eating. Or that he should have packed his vitamins for this trip.

Or why Cyd seemed to have a love-hate relationship with him. He'd prefer more of the former and less of the latter.

He watched Cyd eat. She ate with the gusto of a lumberjack. She'd cut off a slab of meat, stack it with some fries and salad, then shoved the mess into her pretty little mouth and chew with a glazed look that bordered on blissful.

A woman who ate like that could probably kill a man in bed.

Charlie poured another whiskey into Jeffrey's glass. Jeffrey noticed the older guy had a red-white-and-blue peace symbol tattoo on his forearm.

Jeffrey raised the glass, toasted him, then downed the drink. The stuff hit like a hot jolt. Swallowing, hard, he thought back to how just last week he'd been in his New York loft, whipping up his specialty dish—Rock Cornish game hen in apricot sauce—and washing it down with an elegant, buttery chardonnay.

And mere days later, here he was deep in Moose World, numbing himself with mind-altering whiskey.

Charlie leaned closer to Jeffrey. "Brother, I have a cot that can be set up in the back, but my cousin-in-law has dibs on it for tonight. But if you don't mind sleeping with a few dogs, we can throw a sleeping bag in front of the fireplace tonight."

"That'd be great. I have an important radio call in the morning—"

"Wait!" Cyd yelled, her mouth full. She gripped her fork and knife in her fists. She flashed Jeffrey a look that bordered on panic.

Cyd Thompson, panicked? Jeffrey's antennae started waving.

"You can't sleep here, not in *this* room. Those dogs will be *all* over you. By morning, you'll be covered head to toe in their hair—and smell like..." She wrinkled her nose, indicating the word she meant to use.

The lady flies me to the wrong town, and is now concerned about where I sleep?

The concern was compelling.

Too compelling.

Cyd Thompson was definitely up to something, but exactly *what* wasn't yet clear to Jeffrey. Funny how it had always been tougher to read the intentions of someone who had street savvy versus business sharp. Then it hit him how Alaska was just a different version of the streets. A damn sight prettier, but just as tough because it was a world where people had to fight the elements and outwit the beasts to survive.

And that was Cyd to a T. An Alaskan street-savvy woman. No wonder he was having a hell of a time figuring out what she was up to.

"Yes, you'd probably smell pretty damn bad," Charlie concurred with a chuckle, "not to mention you'd be part dog by the mornin'."

Cyd turned her attention to the room. "Hey," she yelled, "anyone got a snowmobile I can borrow? Gotta get to Geraldine's tonight."

Jeffrey was glad he'd just downed a whiskey—it helped him weather the blast of energy Cyd had just emitted. He looked at her perched on that bar stool, her back rigid as she glanced around the room. When had she last combed her hair? It looked like one of those "in" hairdos one saw on the streets of New York, all spiky and sassy. But Jeffrey had no doubt that Cyd's hair was the result of efficiency and practicality. He'd bet she just took a pair of scissors, chopped off a bit here and there, and slapped on a baseball cap.

"You can borrow my machine for a few days," said Harry, sliding a glance from Cyd to Jeffrey and back. "I just loaned it to George, who lives next door."

"And what am I suppos'd to do?" asked a baritone voice, who Jeffrey guessed to be George. "Mine's not fixed yet."

"You got a team and me to cart you wherever you need," Harry answered gruffly.

Jeffrey noticed it was the end of that discussion. If Jeffrey had his group dynamics pegged in this room, Harry was the lead Husky.

Cyd cut off another hunk of meat. "Thanks, Harry." She shoveled some fries and salad onto the meat. "We got a ride to Geri's," she said, glancing at Jeffrey before chomping down on a bite of food that could be a meal unto itself.

He waited until she swallowed. "And there's a place for me to stay at Geri's?" Considering Cyd had promised to take him places before, he didn't want to take anything for granted.

"You got a bed, a roof, free grub."

He fought the urge to smile. He'd had ladies lure him into bedrooms with everything from promises of a "good time" to a bottle of French champagne on ice. But "a bed, a roof, free grub" was a new one.

Of course, Cyd wasn't luring him anywhere...or was she?

"I'll take it," he answered. Better than waking up part dog. "And a ride back here tomorrow morning?"

"No problem," said Cyd sweetly between bites, shooting him that same big-eyed look she'd given him in the radio room.

Which left him wondering why she'd bothered to say the word "no" because he sensed the other word, *problem*, loomed in his immediate future.

3

CYD CUT THE ENGINE of the snowmobile. "We're here," she said. "Time to get off."

Under different circumstances, Jeffrey would have grinned at a lady saying it was time to "get off." But after careening over miles of snow in the gut-chilling Alaskan wilderness with nothing but moonlight as a guide, he wasn't sure if he could even move, much less smile.

Cyd had parked in front of a log cabin, its windows ablaze with light, smoke from the chimney disappearing into the snow-laden sky. An animal's howl punctured the night.

"What's that?" he asked.

"Babette." Cyd leaned over the back of the machine, untying a pouch filled with jerky Harry had insisted she take. Jeffrey hadn't asked, but figured it was in case they got stuck en route.

"Babette?"

"Aunt Geri's dog."

It howled again. A long, mournful sound unlike any dog Jeffrey had known.

He stared at the log cabin, which had at first appeared like some kind of Norman Rockwell painting, but was rapidly taking on the sinister image of a Steven King novel. "Dog? Sounds more like a wolf."

"Wolf?" Cyd muttered something under her breath that sounded like "city slicker." "You better start walking to the cabin. If you keep standing there, your feet will stick to the ice and we'll have to chop them off."

"Anyone ever told you to try stand-up comedy?"

She giggled as she brushed ice off the pouch. "No, but if you're good, maybe I'll sing a few bars."

Her comeback took *him* aback for a moment. Rough and tumble Cyd had a sense of humor, too?

Jeffrey started heading toward the cabin, his feet crunching through the snow. The air smelled smoky, traced with the tang of evergreen. Just as he reached the door, it shook with the weight of something heavy hitting it from the other side. Sniffling and scratching followed, along with a guttural growl.

Jeffrey stared at the door, wondering what the hell he'd gotten himself into. Having street smarts didn't exactly prepare one on how to deal with Cujo.

"Just go in!" Cyd yelled. "Babette's a pussycat."

He looked back at the expanse of moon-glazed, glittering snow that stretched as far as the eye could see. Maybe retracing his steps and having his feet chopped off wasn't such a bad thing.

A huffing, stomping sound distracted him. "Doesn't anybody in New York or L.A. know when to get out of the cold?" With a roll of her eyes, Cyd nudged past him, grabbed the door handle and pushed it open. "Aunt Geri?" she called out.

He followed Cyd inside, blinking into the haze of

light. A woodstove, the fire crackling behind its glass door, sat across the room. The scents of baked bread and coffee wove around him, lulling him out of his mood.

"Hi there, big girl," Cyd cooed, scratching and patting a big, furry head.

He should've known that Cyd and wild beasts would be best pals.

"This is Jeffrey," she said, pointing the furry beast's face at Jeffrey.

"Hi," he said, his eyes adjusting to the light. Babette's yellow eyes took in Jeffrey. She barked, loudly. He put his hand down for her to sniff, hoping she'd eaten something recently. She rubbed her wet nose against his hand, her tail swinging wildly.

Cyd looked up at Jeffrey. "She likes you."

"Good." He'd outwitted death, again. "What kind of dog is she?"

"Mongrel. Part Shepherd, part Husky, and something else."

"Moose?"

Cyd looked at Jeffrey. "City Slicker," she teased, her chocolate brown eyes twinkling.

"Northern Rowdy," he countered.

"Rowdy?" She looked surprised, then burst into laughter. He liked the sound. Loud, infectious. "Sounds about right," she said, pulling the hood of her parka down.

Her face emerged all pink, touched with flakes of snow. Add those devilish brown eyes and wild mass of cropped raven hair, and she looked like sweetness and sin all rolled into one. She was still laughing to herself, repeating the word "rowdy" as she pulled off her parka. Jeffrey felt like leaning over and kissing those pretty lips that curved so deliciously when she smiled. He had the crazy thought that kissing Cyd would be like tasting life itself.

She hung her parka on one of the hooks mounted on the wall next to the front door. "What're you staring at?"

"Your face—" He reached over and brushed some flakes of snow off her cheeks. His gloves were bulky, cold. He pulled them off, tossed them aside and continued brushing her flushed cheeks. Most women needed makeup to look pretty, but not Cyd. Her beauty was like this land. Wild, clean. As though she'd been forged from the sky, the earth.

"We need to get you closer to the fire, warm you up," he said.

She flashed him a look that bordered on shy, which was almost more stunning that her usual tough, don't-mess-with-me attitude. Was she unaccustomed to a man showing tenderness, offering concern for her well-being? A jolt of sadness shot through Jeffrey.

"First, off with our boots," she said softly, looking away. She leaned over and began unlacing hers. "Just toss them here next to the front door."

As Cyd worked on her boots, she called out again, "Aunt Geri?"

Babette barked.

"She'll probably be back in a minute," Cyd commented, pulling off her socks and laying them across her boots. After putting on one of several pairs of slippers piled in a heap on the floor, she walked to the woodstove.

Jeffrey pulled off a wet, heavy boot and looked around the cabin. His first thought was "cozy." His second was "eclectic." The cozy part was the old leather couch topped with a fur pelt, the high-back wooden chairs in front of the woodstove, the multicolored braided rug on the hardwood floor. The eclectic was the assortment of fishing gear and ski equipment in one corner, the pile of miscellaneous tools in another. It was as though someone could walk through the living room and grab whatever they needed on their way out to go fishing, skiing or fixing.

To the left, through a sliding glass door, he spied a glassed-in porch with a covered hot tub. At first he thought the walls were painted white until he realized the glass ceiling and walls were caked with snow.

Cyd stood in front of the woodstove, holding her hands to the heat. She wriggled her toes and moaned pleasurably.

Jeffrey, pulling off his parka, looked up. He hadn't had a quiet minute with her since they'd met, and he took advantage of the moment to look at this little rowdy who had become his cohort. And his opponent, yet she didn't seem so preoccupied with that aspect at the moment.

She looked to be five-four, maybe more, although she had the attitude of someone seven foot. She wore a bulky, white knit sweater with bright red, yellow and pink flowers embroidered along the neckline. Cyd wearing flowers? Not that the sweater wasn't pretty, it's just that flowers seemed so...un-Cyd. She seemed more the type to have wild animals crocheted into her clothes, not dainty blossoms.

Her jeans were faded. And tight. He settled on that compact behind, remembering how it undulated with great purpose as she marched in front of him. It had looked round and firm and...

She turned to warm her backside.

His gaze shot up to her face.

"What're you thinking about?" Cyd asked.

"I, uh, was thinking about things with great purpose."

She ran her hands through her damp hair. "You city types worry too much about the wrong things."

"It's all a matter of semantics."

She stopped fussing with her hair and shot him a look. "Huh?"

"Semantics. How words go together."

She rolled her eyes. "Like I said, you worry about the wrong things."

He laughed, more than willing to let her win this battle. Besides, he liked looking at her taut body. Liked how her wet, black hair had a mind of its own. Unmanageable, wild. *Just like Cyd.* And those lips. Damn if they didn't have the lush pink color of a rose, although she'd probably kill him if she knew he thought that. Hard to believe those rose-petal lips could devour a slab of moose.

She pulled off her bulky sweater.

A hot wave swept through his belly.

She wore a black long-sleeved T-shirt that outlined her breasts just oh so fine. Round, pert...and when she turned just right in the light, he could see the hardened tips of her nipples...

"Now what're you thinking about?" She tossed her sweater over the back of a chair.

He didn't answer. What words could sum up the cascade of feelings that rushed through him, firing his blood? His mind tried to step in and say it was her fault for kick-starting his libido with that rub-a-thon back in the sled basket, but he knew differently. Ever since he'd met Cyd—or more specifically, since he'd realized she wasn't a he—his gut told him he'd met his match. She was sharp, tough and hot.

Sweetly, daringly hot.

The kind of woman you didn't make love to, but with whom you embarked on a fiery sexual adventure.

Cyd held Jeffrey's gaze. Her eyes darkened. Her cheeks flushed crimson. Self-consciously, she turned away and stared at the golden and red flames. "The fire's good," she whispered.

"Sure is," Jeffrey murmured, moving forward and standing next to her. Far away enough to give her room, show her respect. Close enough to sense her heat, catch her scent. Fresh and sweet, the way the world smelled after a spring rain.

They stood side by side, the only sound the crackling of the fire. Babette lay on the edge of the hearth, next to a bone and a plastic squeaky toy that had seen better days.

When Cyd slid Jeffrey a sideways glance, he saw

how her long, black eyelashes cast spiky shadows on her cheeks. Caught a look of longing in her eyes that flamed his needs even higher. Was she feeling what he felt? Or did she view him as another of her competitions. Maybe that was what was behind some of her antagonistic actions. She was accustomed to competing, not communing with guys.

If so, tonight he'd let her win. He'd let her have anything if she'd reward him with a kiss, a touch…

He blinked and turned his gaze to the flames. *What in the hell am I thinking? I'm here on* business *not pleasure.* Top priority is to research Arctic Luck, then fly back to L.A. tomorrow. *The last thing I need to think about is a roll in the sack with Cyd.* One hundred percent of his focus needed to be on Monday morning's meeting, which would cinch him a promotion and a better career if he played his cards right.

He cleared his throat, as though that would clear his mind, and looked around for something to distract his libido. His gaze landed on an assortment of pictures on the wall. Several photos were of a burly man and a woman, who appeared to be outdoors, some school pictures of children, and a large group photo.

The latter, especially, drew his attention. He stepped forward for a better look.

"Is this you?" he asked incredulously, pointing to a young girl with long black hair curled prettily around her shoulders.

"Yes."

He would have recognized those big chocolate brown eyes anywhere, but not the dress, the long styled hair. Interesting. Whereas he'd gone from street tough to executive, she'd gone from sweet girl to tough independent. They'd both started out one way, and somewhere along the road of life, taken a sharp one-eighty.

He wondered what her one-eighty was...and why they chose almost completely different paths. But even if they'd ended up in such different lifestyles, they shared a fundamental knowledge about survival that one learned only on the streets or in the wilderness.

Maybe the city slicker and the northern rowdy weren't so different, after all.

"When was this picture taken?" he asked.

"When I was fourteen."

Jeffrey stared intently at the picture, then back to Cyd. "It's not in Alaska."

"Seattle."

"You look very happy."

"I was."

Cyd stared at the picture, remembering how life had been way back when. How her dad loved managing the movie theater, and how her mom laughed a lot, even though she spent most of her time chasing down two toddlers, Cyd's younger siblings. Cyd, being older and being her daddy's girl, had spent her free time tagging along with him to the theater, watching him thread the big reels of film or helping out at the ticket booth and snack bar.

She didn't like the memories that had just been resurrected. Memories of a sweeter life, one where her family had been whole.

She stared at Jeffrey, long and hard, fighting more memories. How her dad changed when he lost his theater to some big-business movie chain. He'd always been such a fun, gregarious guy, but after he'd had to close down the theater, he'd grown tired, sadder. Then one day he moved his family to Alaska, the last "safe place in the world" her dad had claimed.

And then...

She didn't want to think about that.

"I don't want your film series to come to Alaska," she blurted.

The front door creaked open.

A big body, swathed in an even bigger blue coat, clumped into the room. Babette leaped to her feet and started barking energetically, her tail thumping double-time. The person stopped, took one look at Cyd and opened her arms wide. "Sweetie girl!"

With a laugh, Cyd rushed forward into the hug. After some back-thumping and greetings, Cyd turned to Jeffrey. "This is my aunt Geri. Geri, Jeffrey."

"Jeffrey," Geri said with a smile, removing her beaver cap. A long silver braid fell over her shoulder. "Nice to meet ya." She pulled off a red mitten and shook his hand heartily. She gave Babette a rub behind the ear.

Geri's gray eyes glistened in a way that made Cyd nervous. She only looked that way before a fishing or hunting expedition. And it sure didn't seem any such expedition was taking place at this hour of the night.

But then Cyd had never shown up with a guy before. And ever since her dad—Geri's baby brother—had died, Geri had often talked about Cyd building her own family someday. Didn't Geri realize that Cyd had enough on her hands filling her dad's shoes? Helping out financially, ensuring her siblings stayed on the right path?

Geri removed her wool coat. "Ran by the neighbor's, made sure he had enough firewood." She pulled off her boots, then crossed to the woodstove, where she began warming herself. "You remember Calvin, Cyd?"

"That old guy next door?"

Geri raised her eyebrows. "Sixty-two isn't *that* old." She looked from Cyd to Jeffrey. "Hungry? I got some bread, bacon, moose steaks."

"No, thanks," Jeffrey said quickly.

"We ate at the Mush," explained Cyd.

"So what brings you kids on this surprise visit?"

"Business," Cyd said tightly. *Big business that she'd put a stop to come hell or high water.*

Jeffrey nodded.

Geri swung her long braid back over her shoulder, assessing both of them. "I see," she said quietly, her gaze taking in Jeffrey's pin-striped shirt and creased slacks. Her gaze traveled to his hands, which he held palms out to the fire. She smiled.

"Say!" she suddenly exclaimed. "You two've probably had a long trip, eh? A nice, steamy hot tub works wonders on tired muscles."

"Uh, no, thanks," murmured Cyd.

Jeffrey scratched his chin. "It's late. I'll pass."

"Well, it's just out the sliding glass door on the porch, so help yourself if the mood strikes."

There was such a long stretch of silence, Cyd wondered if Jeffrey had had the same mood strike that she'd had earlier. Had to be that damn sled basket. Ever since they'd been packed tightly in there, some kind of sizzling current had been zapping back and forth between them. She'd take Jeffrey back to the plane on a snowmobile.

"It's late, Aunt Geri. I think we'll just go to bed, if that's okay."

"Certainly, sweetie. Which bed you takin'?"

Cyd felt the blood race to her cheeks again. "I'm sharing your bed, of course!" she said a bit too quickly. "He can sleep on the fold-out couch, alone, out here."

"Oh, right, this is a *business* trip. Forgot." Geri smiled benevolently at Jeffrey. "Let me get some sheets and blankets, make up the couch."

But as her aunt bustled out of the room, Cyd knew in her gut that Geri hadn't forgotten this was a business trip. Geri never forgot anything. She was like a walking encyclopedia.

Unless Cyd was seriously mistaken, her aunt was definitely on a hunting expedition.

Determined to hunt down a husband for Cyd.

JEFFREY WOKE UP TO THE SMELL of coffee and bacon frying. At first he thought he was at his condo in L.A. and wondered why his housekeeper was frying *bacon*. Breakfast was typically oatmeal, fruit, maybe some cheese slices or tofu. But *bacon?* Never.

"Good morning, Jeff!" Geri stepped into the living room from the kitchen doorway, a spatula in her hand. She stood in front of the far window, her blue gray flannel shirt blending into the overcast scenery outside.

The "Jeff" took him by surprise. The only person who ever abbreviated his name was his best pal Rob.

"Morning, Geri," he answered. She was definitely a Geri, not the "Geraldine" Cyd had referred to at the lodge. Maybe, like Jeffrey, most people used her full name because it was respectful. And from what he'd seen of her, this was definitely a lady to respect.

"Told Calvin I'd drop by some bread, so I need to leave in a minute. Left some grub on the stove for you and Cyd."

This was almost like having a mom. Or how he, as a kid, had imagined a mom to be. Bustling about in the kitchen, always happy to see you.

Not how it had really been in the foster homes he'd been dropped into. In those places, he always felt uncomfortable, knowing those people were paid to care for him, not paid to love him. Early on, he'd been jealous of kids who knew how it felt to be part of a family, but that mood passed. By the time he was sixteen, he made the streets his family. And he got more camaraderie, more "love" if you will, from newspaper vendors and bar owners than he ever had from some foster home.

"That's very affable of you," he responded to Geri's offer of food.

"Affa—?" she hooted. "You not only look fancy, you

talk fancy, too." She paused. "Don't get me wrong. I like it, Jeff."

He smiled, scraping a hand across his face, feeling the day's growth of beard he never allowed. "I'll be leaving this morning, so I'd like to thank you for your hospitality."

"This morning?" She glanced behind her at the swirls of falling snow. "Weather don't look so good."

"Well, that's what they say, but Jordan's going to work something out."

"Oh." But Geri didn't look convinced. "Well, have a safe trip, Jeff." She paused. "Cyd's a great girl, you know."

His antennae started waving. "Uh, yes, she is."

"You're not married, right?"

Being matchmaked first thing in the morning was more stunning for a man than a quart of caffeine fed intravenously. He felt like crushing the issue by saying that Cyd was more into love-hate with him, not love, but knew better than to pursue this particular discussion more than necessary.

Instead he murmured, "Uh, no."

"Like kids?"

"Other people's, yes."

"You'll get over that. Which city you from?"

Get over what? "Uh, New York. And Los Angeles." He was never at a loss for words, but Geri was putting the fear of God into him. Did they have shotgun weddings in Alaska?

"Two big cities, eh?" She trundled back into the

kitchen, then returned minus the spatula. "Well, life's about choices, isn't it?"

She bustled over to the wall hooks and removed her coat, beaver cap and gloves. She started putting them on.

"What choices?" Cyd stumbled sleepily into the living room, an oversize gray-and-red patterned robe wrapped around her.

Jeffrey tried not to give her a once-over, but he'd never seen a woman look so deliciously sexy wearing nothing but a man's robe. She'd pulled the sash tight, which emphasized the smallness of her waist. And, above, the fullness of her breasts. The way they pressed provocatively against the material made him want to be reborn a piece of flannel.

"Just tellin' Jeffrey how I need to drop off some bread to Calvin. Breakfast's in the kitchen," Geri said nonchalantly, walking heavily in her outdoor gear back into the kitchen.

With a yawn, Cyd looked at Jeffrey. "Mornin'."

He loved Cyd's voice in the morning. All husky and sleepy. He thought how that voice would sound in the dark, murmuring words of lust.

And she sounded...sweet. As though there was nothing better in the world than to wish a "good morning" to Jeffrey.

"Mornin'," he murmured, fighting images of naked bodies in twisted bedsheets.

Cyd took a step forward and squinted. "That's some beard you got working there." She grinned. That devilish grin that could give Meg Ryan a run for her money.

"Your aunt have a razor I can borrow?"

Cyd shook her head side to side. "Even if she did, I wouldn't let you use it. You're cute with some growth on your face. Makes you look...rugged."

The way she stared at him, damn near moaning the word "rugged" almost made him swear to never shave again for the rest of his life. What was this new side of Cyd? He was fairly sure she wasn't into shotgun weddings the way her aunt seemed to be, but Cyd was into something...

He had a little time to work this one out, figure out what's what. Meanwhile, he'd just enjoy how Cyd had evolved from Amelia Earhart to a pixie-cut Catherine Zeta-Jones.

He liked that. He'd never met a woman who could be one of the guys on the outside, and one hell of a woman on the inside, too. His eyes trailed up her bare legs to the point where they disappeared underneath the robe.

He was thinking about what was beneath that red-and-gray fabric when Geri burst from the kitchen with a bag in her hands.

"On my way to Calvin's. Babette's fed, sound asleep in the kitchen. Cyd, sweetie girl, will I see you later?"

"Of course. We're weathered in."

Jeffrey thought Cyd sounded a bit too happy announcing that bit of news.

Geri flashed Jeffrey a look. "Oh. Well, I'll be back in two to three hours."

"Two to three?" asked Cyd. "How long does it take to drop off some bread?"

Geri headed to the front door. "Snow's deep. Roads are blocked. Temperature's at least twenty below."

"He lives in the *next* cabin, a couple hundred yards away, tops!" Cyd looked baffled.

"I'm being affable." As Geri opened the front door, she winked at Jeffrey. "Cyd needs to understand the finer things in life. Maybe you can help."

The door shut behind her with a resounding thud.

AFTER BREAKFAST, which consisted of toast and coffee for Jeffrey, and bacon, eggs, toast, a poppy seed muffin and enough coffee to stun a moose, Cyd brushed the crumbs from her face and robe, then sighed contentedly. "That'll hold me till lunch."

That would be enough to hold Jeffrey until the next millennium, but he kept the thought to himself.

Picking up some dirty dishes, he asked, "When are we leaving for the Mush Lodge? I need to radio Jordan, hear his plans for getting me back to L.A. I have to pitch the series tomorrow morning, and I can't be late."

Cyd pursed her lips, then spoke. "I need to get dressed first."

She sounded a bit defensive. "Didn't expect you to drive that snowmobile naked," he countered.

"Wouldn't be the first time."

He dropped a dish, which clattered onto the counter. In the corner, Babette raised her head.

"You okay?" asked Cyd.

Hell no. "I'm fine," Jeffrey muttered, fighting images

of a naked Cyd on a snowmobile, all creamy and pink. His groin tightened, so he busied himself stacking and restacking plates and cups so he could stay facing the kitchen sink and not turn around.

"You this neat at home?"

"Thought you were getting dressed," he said thickly.

"I'm finishing my coffee." She paused. "You didn't answer my question."

"Am I what? Neat?"

"You know, picking up things, stacking things."

Only when I have a raging hard-on. He rinsed some silverware. "Yeah, sure, I'm neat." If he stayed around Cyd too long, he could start a second career as a professional housekeeper.

He sensed a shift in the room. He glanced to his left and saw her standing close, her big eyes all round and moist. That look made his antennae go on alert.

"You're quite the little actress, aren't you?"

"Me, really?" She set her cup on the counter. "I'll go get dressed now."

The ticking of the kitchen clock sliced off the seconds.

"Good idea," he murmured, wondering what the hell she was up to. She'd blurted last night that she didn't want a TV series here in Alaska, made it even clearer she wasn't exactly fond of city-slicker types, so why was she turning up the heat?

"Damn!" she exclaimed.

He nearly dropped a plate again. "What?"

"Where are the snowmobile keys?"

Babette barked.

"You drove last night—what'd you do with them?"

"I hung them on the key hook over the sink." Cyd pointed to a nail above the chipped porcelain bowl. "They're gone."

Jeffrey looked at the nail, which obviously doubled as the "key hook." "Maybe Geri took them by mistake?"

Cyd batted her eyes, something she'd seen Meryl Streep do in almost every romantic film she ever starred in. Cyd hoped her eye-batting made it look as though she thought Jeffrey had just said the most brilliant thing in the world.

"You're so smart," she cooed. Hopefully, not too smart. She didn't want him figuring out what she'd done.

"Yeah," grumbled Jeffrey. "Probably grabbed the keys, not realizing hers were already in her pocket, and now *both* sets of keys are at Calvin's."

Great. This is exactly what she wanted Jeffrey to think. Geri had taken the keys, he was stuck here. She'd hoped her aunt would be gone longer than a few hours, but at least a few hours meant that much longer before Jeffrey did his big-business radio call...and she was determined to do anything to thwart his big-business plans.

Even playing sex siren this morning, which was a bigger challenge than racing the Fairbanks Flight during that blizzard. But whatever it took, she'd win this competition with Jeffrey. Hell, she was winning for Alaska!

"Damn!" Jeffrey slammed his fist on the counter.

"What?"

"It's *imperative* I speak to Jordan this morning."

"No problem," Cyd said sweetly. Eww, even she didn't like that syrupy sound in her voice. "Geri will be back soon."

"Two to three hours."

"Your call will be a little late, that's all."

"Two to three *hours* is more than a *little* late."

"I'm sorry," Cyd said, moving closer. "I know how important that call is for you." She wondered if he smelled the vanilla she'd dabbed behind her ears earlier. It was the best she could do for perfume at a moment's notice.

"Can't we call Calvin, have Geri come back?"

Cyd shrugged apologetically. "He doesn't have a phone," she said, mustering all the sadness she could in her voice.

"No phone? What kind of place is this!"

"You're in the last frontier," Cyd explained calmly. "Life is rougher, tougher out here." *Like the women.*

"Obviously you've never been to L.A." Jeffrey gave his head a shake. "This is a disaster."

"Hey." Cyd took his hand and squeezed it. She paused, trying not to think how big and warm his hand felt. Or how their fingers comfortably intertwined, as though they were a natural fit. "You're, uh, getting awfully stressed. I know just the antidote." Finally, the moment she'd been waiting for. The ultimate technique to take Jeffrey's mind off business.

Jeffrey raised his head and sniffed. "Did someone

spill vanilla?" He began looking around the floor, as though he expected to find a pool of it lying someplace.

Cyd took the opportunity to doff her robe, tossing it over the back of a kitchen chair.

Jeffrey straightened and turned around. "Doesn't appear anything spilled—"

Honest to God, she'd never seen a man stare at her like that. His eyes all liquid and shiny. Was that a look of excitement or shock? Damn, had she overdone it?

I must win. I must win.

She placed her hands behind her head, the way she'd seen that girl in her dad's pinup poster do. For extra effect, Cyd thrust out one hip. That girl in the pinup poster had also worn high heels, a girly item Cyd had never owned, so she compensated by standing just a little bit on the balls of her feet.

Jeffrey's gaze traveled along her arms, over her breasts, to that thrust-out hip, then back to her eyes.

"What in the hell are you doing?" he said in a choked voice.

"Taking a hot tub," she answered, trying her damnedest to sound coy and suggestive. Still holding her hands on her head, she swiveled ever so slowly and began walking out of the kitchen toward the tub, straining to hear Jeffrey's footsteps behind her.

Something clunked. A soft curse.

She winced, realizing she should have told him about that raised floorboard. But the good news was that he was following her.

She smiled.

Her plan was in effect, headed for success.

4

JEFFREY STUMBLED FORWARD, catching himself before he kissed the scuffed hardwood floor between the kitchen and living room. He glanced behind him and spied the buckled floorboard. He blew out a gust of breath. *Like hell it was a floorboard that made me lose my equilibrium.*

I lost it over Cyd.

He looked up in time to see she'd wrapped a fur—the one that had been lying across the old leather couch—around her pink nakedness. Hidden beneath the sensuous wrap were all those sweet indentations and curves that had reduced him to a stumbling fool.

He scrubbed a hand across his face, willing himself to keep it together. After all, he had no lack of female companionship—in fact, his buddies often kidded him that the quantity of numbers in his black book could impress the New York Stock Exchange.

But just as the exchange was about business, so were Jeffrey's dates. Blame it on his growing up in foster homes, or a stellar crash-and-burn engagement five years ago, but he'd decided his life worked much better without emotional entanglements. Women were arm candy, he was a generous date, and all in all it was a sweet deal.

Simple. Tidy. Efficient.

But with Cyd, everything felt different.

Complex.

Chaotic.

And the way he'd just stumbled over a floorboard, clumsy. This little dynamo had thrown his world off balance. And he *never* felt off-balance.

Well, until he landed in Alaska.

He recalled her words from last evening. *I don't want your film series to come to Alaska.* Was *that* what this was about? For some cockamamie reason, did she think sex would somehow stop his plans for the series?

Time to put the brakes on this rustic seduction. Get things back on track. Show her who was in control.

He opened his mouth to say something along these lines, but when their gazes caught, all he could think was how that damn fur hid the prettiest breasts he'd ever seen.

Like hell I'm in control.

Her eyes darkened as though she read his thoughts. A faint smile tipped her lips.

And damn if his didn't slide into a grin.

Her smile widened. So wide and generous, it could almost be labeled wholesome. Almost. Considering her naked-under-a-fur status, it was *wickedly* wholesome.

They stood staring at each other, grinning like two lunatics. And in a crazy moment, he felt happy. Illogically, irrationally happy for no other reason than it felt good to be here, to be experiencing out-of-control, hot feelings.

It felt good to be with Cyd.

"I'm getting into the hot tub," she said, breaking the silence. "Care to join me?"

His head filled with images of slippery skin against skin, limbs intertwining under bubbling water. And with a yearning that bordered on painful, he ached to kiss her, taste her, sink himself deep in her...

Don't lose control. Your entire career hinges on that radio call.

If he didn't speak with Jordan soon, arrange a flight to L.A., he could screw up his golden opportunity at tomorrow's board meeting. It had taken months to plan this meeting, get the key people to assemble in one city, one room. Some lived in L.A., but others lived out of state. The chairman of the board, Harold Gauthier, was flying in via private jet from France. It was the most critical gathering of the year for the Argonaut Studios leaders because decisions made tomorrow shaped the company's future.

And one of those key decisions would be, based on Jeffrey's presentation, whether the studio would finance his Alaskan film series. And, more importantly, give him the promotion.

If he screwed it up, he'd screw up his own promotion as well as jobs for hundreds of people. He couldn't chance taking a "hot tub time-out" and losing sense of time altogether.

"Can't join you," he rasped.

She tilted her head. "Not even a little dip? It feels so good on achy muscles..."

The way she said "achy" triggered seismic tremors through him.

"Plus you were traveling all day yesterday," she murmured. "A hot tub would be *so* relaxing."

Her plump lips formed the sweetest little "o" when she said "so." *Radio-call. Board meeting.* "Can't."

"Can't? Or *won't?*" She let the fur open just enough to reveal the soft curve of her mounds and a hint of shadowy cleavage. "You city types work way too hard. You need to learn to take it easy, reward yourselves."

He imagined rewarding himself by yanking off that damn fur and taking her, hard and fast, right here on the floor. He started to surge forward.

And stopped himself.

I don't want your film series to come to Alaska.

"Can't." He swallowed, hard. "No time."

"No time," she repeated softly, saying the words as though they were foreign, unrecognizable.

He caught another whiff of vanilla and realized the stuff hadn't spilled in the kitchen...it had spilled on Cyd's heated body. His mind reeled with thoughts of sniffing—and sucking and licking—the sweet concoction off her skin.

Vanilla.

Naked under fur.

He'd never known a woman who made the wild, natural elements so damn exotic. These Alaskan women knew how to do it right.

"Well," she said, her voice dropping to a sultry timbre, "you don't mind if *I* take the time, do you?" Not waiting for an answer, Cyd pivoted and walked away. With each step, the fur slipped a little, gradually revealing the taut planes of her back, the curve of her waist.

Like a fallen sailor lured by the song of the Sirens, he followed her, vaguely aware of the crackling fire in the woodstove, the lingering scent of morning coffee, the distant ticking of the kitchen clock.

Cyd reached the glass door to the deck and clicked it open. Lowering him a look over her bare shoulder, she said, "Geri keeps this door closed because Babette either chews on the tub cover or if someone's taken that off, makes a flying leap into the water."

Jeffrey nodded, pretending to listen, but the words were having a hell of a time getting through the visual. Cyd's full lips, the curve of her shoulder, those shapely legs.

She held open the door, arching one eyebrow. Maybe before he thought she looked wickedly wholesome, but now she just looked wicked. Sinfully, deliciously wicked.

The air sizzled with anticipation. He shifted his weight, anxious, ready. A single touch could ignite an inferno.

Her eyes veiled with sexual arousal, Cyd stared at him...then quickly stepped inside and closed the sliding glass door. It clicked shut, the sound reverberating through the room.

She cut me off.

He was momentarily stunned. And irritated. Nobody ever shut him out. Nobody dared. Jeffrey was fair, but tough, and one thing he didn't condone was insubordination or rudeness.

Of course, she hadn't really been either. Well, a little rude considering she'd neatly short-circuited an electrical storm. But the truth was, in her own take-it-or-leave-it way, she'd issued an ultimatum. He didn't take it, so he was shut out.

Damn if she didn't intrigue him all the more. Because without a word, she'd just told him she didn't give a flying hoot about his power or money. And based on her comment that she didn't want his series coming to Alaska, it appeared she was willing to play tough with anything at her disposal to keep his power and money away from her world.

She was wrong, of course.

He still didn't understand what the hell her issues were, but when he got his wits back, he'd ask her questions, figure out the problem, then explain how his ideas and Arctic Luck's needs were a perfect fit. A win-win combination. Yes, the problem was manageable. She'd been stuck out here away from civilization too long, that's all. Couldn't see the forest for the trees. After he resolved his flight home, he'd enlighten her. Didn't want to leave any roadblocks behind when he left for L.A.

He watched her through the glass as she soundlessly walked around the sunken tub. Hazy sunlight filtered through the snow-caked walls, casting the room in an ethereal blue. It was almost like watching a dream. A gorgeous woman, tinged in magic, wearing nothing but a lush pelt.

Gripping the fur around her with one hand, she

lifted the cover off the tub effortlessly with her other, and with a flick of her wrist, flipped it out of the way.

Dexterous, isn't she.

But when he recalled her landing that plane on a strip of dirt, not such a big surprise.

She dipped one foot into the water and wriggled her toes. Glancing at him, she laughed, the sound muted.

A rush of memory invaded his thoughts. He'd been sixteen. Winter night in Philly. Weather so cold, it stabbed straight through clothes.

It had been late, after ten. He'd been walking home from the Dew Drop Inn, a downtown pub that was more home than his foster one. He spent most evenings at the pub, chatting with the regulars, eating food the owner set in front of him. In between, he'd finish homework, read a novel.

Then he'd walk home to meet his eleven o'clock curfew. On frigid nights, he had a trick to keep his mind occupied on something other than the weather. He'd repeat a snippet of dialogue or text from the novel he was currently reading. He'd play with the words, turn them this way and that as he shouldered his way through the brisk chill.

That night, he'd just turned down a side street when a movement caught his eye. He'd looked up at an apartment window, its drapes open, and halted.

The words he'd been reciting disappeared in a release of mist from his breath.

Through the window, he saw the apartment was mostly dark except for a hazy slant of light from a hallway. Within the layered shadows, a woman was undressing. He couldn't distinguish her features, or even the color of her hair except that it fell in loose waves to her shoulders.

She was leaning over, stepping out of a slip. Her legs were stocky, yet the movements dainty. She tossed the filmy undergarment, which sifted into the dark.

Then she unhooked her bra and slowly peeled if off. As she turned to toss the bra, he saw her breasts in a slant of light. Heavy with dark tips.

By then, he'd been with a few girls. Heated gropes, flash point releases. But standing alone on a sidewalk late at night, the window became a portal to another world. One where sex merged with sensuality. The erotic act of a woman purposefully, seductively removing her clothes. Waves of explosive currents raced through him.

And then she looked at him, the curves of her body creating a titillating pattern of light and dark.

He'd stood there, spellbound. His body on fire. And he'd known that all he had to do was walk up to that window and she'd let him inside...

Then, it started to snow.

Fat flakes of white filled the space between him and the window.

He'd turned and continued walking home.

To this day, he still didn't know why he'd stepped away from the fantasy. Sometimes he wondered if he feared the fantasy could never live up to the reality.

All these years later, standing outside a glass partition with Cyd on the inside playing her toes in the water, he felt like that kid again. Awestruck. Tormented.

But instead of peering into shadows, he could clearly see the longhaired, red-tinged fur and how it set fire to her pink-gold skin. How the silky hairs teased the soft mounds of her breasts and skirted the top of her shapely thighs. He yearned for her to remove that fur, slowly, and reveal herself to him.

And in his heart he knew that this time, the fantasy wouldn't outweigh the reality.

This time, he wouldn't walk away.

Cyd looked down at the swirling blue green water in the sunken hot tub and swished her toes in it, wondering what the hell to do next. Good thing Geri kept this room heated, too, so she wasn't freezing her tootsies— or anything else—off out here.

Going butt naked in the kitchen had been pure—or not so pure—inspiration. Anyway, being naked was no big deal. Half of Arctic Luck—Katimuk, too—had seen her in the buff last summer when she skinny-dipped at the Fourth of July community picnic.

After traipsing naked out of the kitchen a few minutes ago, she'd spied the fur and got inspired again. And she knew her inspiration had hit gold when Jeffrey's eyes burned brighter. She'd never thought of herself as a femme fatale, but seeing Jeffrey get so hot and bothered filled her with a delicious sense of power.

She smiled to herself, swishing her foot in the bubbles. She dug that feeling of power. If only she could continue successfully enticing him from his urgency to get on that damn snowmobile and head to the Mush Lodge.

Her smile dropped.

But what to do next? How could she top the naked-under-the-fur bit?

If he was a Northern boy, Cyd would've pounced him in the kitchen where they would have christened the stove, the kitchen sink, then worked their way across the braided rug, and now be ready to tackle the tub.

But this was different. She had to divert Jeffrey's attention indefinitely. Get him to forget about that damn radiophone at the Mush Lodge. Because no way in hell did she want him talking to Jordan.

It wasn't that Jordan could finagle a plane in this weather, but with his recent customer service obsession, he might offer Jeffrey more free trips around Alaska. Just what the state needed, a big-business city slicker mucking around, flying here and there, sticking his moneyed fingers into other people's business. He'd change their lives for the worse, taint the fierce beauty of their frontier.

The other scenario was that Jeffrey—after being told *again* by Jordan that no transportation to L.A. was available—might take it upon himself to radiophone someone else to negotiate on his behalf or whatever bigwigs did when they couldn't "take a meeting." And some faceless threat would start the wheels turning for that damn series up here.

Yes, her best plan was to methodically seduce Jeffrey, keep him hotly occupied. *Give him cabin fever.* And if her aunt walked in on them, well, Geri would be thrilled to see Cyd and Jeffrey were getting along so well.

Cyd peeked a look through the glass at Jeffrey's flushed, confused expression. *He's wondering why I'm ignoring him. I've been toe-dipping and thinking too long. Time to get this act in gear and do more femme fatale stuff.*

What would a city girl do?

Well, so far the taking-it-slow fur-thing had worked. She'd do more of the same.

Straightening, Cyd looked out the window and saw Jeffrey's look shift from confused to a subtle wariness.

Not good. He's coming out of the sexy haze. Need to lure him in here...get him into the tub. Lots of time—hours— could be spent soaking and lusting. And then, later, Cyd could sweetly say it's just too darn late to head out to the Mush. Maybe tell a few stories of bears eating people on snowmobiles. Oh, yeah, that'd be a good story for a city guy.

That is, if a snowmobile were even available. Which would only happen if Geri let him borrow hers because, despite Jeffrey's belief, her aunt hadn't accidentally taken the keys to Calvin's.

With a surge of renewed confidence, she wriggled her shoulders, letting the fur shimmy lower until it slipped off one breast. The onslaught of cool air made her nipple pucker.

Jeffrey's mouth parted. But he didn't move. At least that wary look was gone. But damn, you'd think the guy was frozen to that spot on the rug. *What is it with these city boys?* Any red-blooded Alaskan hunk would be bolting through the door, ready to stake a claim.

He's thinking about the radio call. Got to lure him in here.

Fighting the urge to drop the damn fur in one fell

swoop, Cyd inched it down until both breasts were un-
covered. They felt perky, achy, and she locked her gaze
with Jeffrey, daring him to break glass.

Nothing.

Damn, this man moved slower than a glacier.

When he had the wherewithal to look up from staring at her mounds, she smiled. For added effect, she
flicked her tongue along her lower lip.

His eyes widened. His hands clenched into tight
balls.

Then...nothing.

She drew in a deep breath, making her breasts swell.
He took a step forward.

Progress!

She did the same, taking a slow step toward the
glass, her fingers clutching the soft, lush fur around her
waist.

They both stopped, staring at each other.

And then Cyd got it. *This is like a game of chess.* A calculated dance of seduction. Of course Jeffrey didn't immediately lunge for her. This wasn't the kind of man
who, at the first flash of desire, rushed to stake a claim.
This was a man who was accustomed to the games of
big business.

Such a man would undoubtedly like things complex.
After all, what was the thrill in winning a game with no
rules? No challenges?

She might be a northern rowdy, but piloting planes
had taught her to quickly assess situations, make rapid
decisions. Her analytical nature came in handy with

people, too. Most of the time, she was right on in sizing them up, determining how to proceed.

Maybe before she'd felt clueless about how to be a femme fatale, how to compete with city girls, but now she knew that wasn't the issue at all. She just had to play the game Jeffrey's way, stimulate his body *and* his mind. Make the prize worthwhile.

She turned her back, letting the fur slide down, down until it slipped past her rump. Her skin prickled as cool air caressed her bottom. For extra effect, she gave it a little wiggle as though to say "here it is." In her mind's eye, she imagined his reaction. More heat rushing to his face, shoving a hand through his hair as though disbelieving what she was pulling now.

She loved it. *City girls, eat your hearts out!*

Cyd still held the fur closed together over her hips, covering her most secret part. She turned sideways, checked him out. Oh, yeah, she'd been right on. The color flooding his cheeks made his eyes blaze greener than usual. And his hair was hopelessly mussed. He must have speared his anxious fingers through the mass as though it would help him gather his thoughts.

And surprise, surprise, he'd popped open several buttons at the neck of his blue-and-white striped shirt as though it might help him breath better.

She faced him full on, watching his gaze roam hotly over her body, waiting for her next move.

This was a hell of a lot more fun than her usual pouncing maneuver. Teasing him slowly had an additional perk in that she could gauge her feelings, too. And right now, Cyd felt *desirable.* As though she were on stage, entertaining her audience of one, expertly manipulating his reactions with erotically calculated moves.

Wow. Heady stuff.

Heat spiraled through her and she realized this steamy act was stroking her libido, too. Big time. Her pulse pounded in her ears, drowning out the gentle bubbling of the hot tub.

Time to up the stakes.

She pulled open the edges of the fur a few inches, holding the wrap open slightly, just enough to offer a teasing glimpse of skin and shadow. As his eyes lowered, heat flooded her, pooling to the spot he looked at.

Jeffrey's mouth went dry as he stared at Cyd, holding open the pelt, displaying herself to him.

And then she dropped the covering.

She stood naked, her taut form rising above the pile of luxurious fur. Like an untamed Botticelli's Venus.

The light sifting through the snow glazed her with a shimmering blue. Touches of black grounded the picture. Her black, wild hair. Those chocolate eyes. And the triangle of dark curls around her sex.

His heart thundered over the distant ticking of the kitchen clock and he had the sense time was slipping away. But the sight of her naked lusciousness and the come-hither look in her eyes dispersed his thoughts like vapor from breath on a cold night.

Cyd stepped closer to the glass.

One corner of her lips quirked upward as she pressed her hands against the slick surface and stared at him as though to say "What are you waiting for?"

With a soft curse, he pitched forward and pressed his hand flat against the glass, his fingers pulsing as though virtually fondling a breast.

She leaned closer, touching a dusty pink tip to the pane where his hand lay, the bud tightening upon impact. Moisture emanated from his fingers as he stroked a circle around the flattened nipple.

Arching her back, Cyd mouthed his name, the warmth of her breath steaming the glass.

A deep, hungry sound reverberated in his throat. Heat blasted through him, spinning him out of control. *Have to get to her.*

He turned, yanked on the door handle and shoved the glass door open. Stepping inside, mist rushed at him, the air drenched with steam and female scent.

Cyd, her eyes big and wide, stepped back.

"You're not going anywhere," he growled, tugging at the buttons on his shirt.

Her gaze darted at the movements of his hands flying over buttons, yanking the shirt tails out of his pants. Color flamed her skin as her lips parted.

Sensations rocked through him as he fumbled with the last buttons on his shirt. *To hell with it.* He ripped the shirt the rest of the way off, buttons popping, pinging against glass. He was hard, on fire, and she'd pushed it too far.

"Come here." With a growl, he grabbed her wrists and tugged her closer. Manacled in his grip, he plastered her body against him, pressing those swollen breasts against his chest. Lust and desire and need coalesced into a single blazing imperative as he shoved his knee between her legs, forcing them apart.

"Damn...you're...hot," he breathed, moving her wrists, causing her body to sway so her hardened tips brushed against his chest. Where their skin touched, fires erupted, burning down to his groin.

Lowering his head, he touched his lips to her soft, panting mouth. "I'm going to take you right here—"

A loud creak. Stomping noises. Babette barking.

"I'm home!" yelled Geri.

5

CYD YANKED THE FUR OFF the floor and slung it around herself. "Aunt Geri, we're in the tub—"

The *clunk clunk clunk* of heavy boots preceded Geri appearing in front of the glass doors. She was leaning over, scratching Babette, whose tail was thumping wildly. "Yes, you're a good girl," Geri cooed. After a last pat on the dog's head, Geri looked up.

And froze.

So did Jeffrey. In the last few moments, he'd managed to grab his shirt and shove a fist through a sleeve. Now he stood, bare-chested, one arm frozen midshove, the rest of the shirt dangling.

Geri looked at his shirt, stared longer at his chest, then met his eyes.

He twisted a smile. "Welcome home," he murmured, then squeezed shut his eyes as he debated if he should just kick himself now or later for thinking such an inane greeting glossed over the fact that his host had just caught him in a compromising situation with her niece.

He opened his eyes, determined not to speak again during this bizarre encounter. He didn't trust his brain and tongue to work in tandem and say something reasonably intelligent.

Geri's gaze wandered over to Cyd, whose pelt hung at an angle.

"Uh, we were just getting into the tub," Cyd said in an elaborately casual voice.

Something in all that fur caught Jeffrey's eye. He glanced down. One of Cyd's breasts had escaped. The creamy, pink-tipped mound stuck out for all the world—and Geri—to see.

Geri's eyes dipped and returned to Cyd's face. So she hadn't missed the errant body part either.

"Uh-huh," Geri said, nodding.

Babette was nosing around the doorway, keenly sniffing an object.

"What you find there, girl?" Geri bent over and picked up a small object. She held it up and frowned. "A button?"

Geri looked from it to Jeffrey's shirt. "Uh-huhhh," she said again, drawing out the sounds until it sounded like an entire sentence. Worse, a smile that looked oddly triumphant creased her face.

Damn if heat didn't rush to Jeffrey's face as though he were some teenage kid caught in the throes of delinquent passion. It had been years since he'd felt this way. But now the memory of being caught in the back seat of a Cadillac, which belonged to the girl's father, came rushing back as though it were yesterday. Steamed-up windows, tangled clothes, the only difference being the father was red-faced angry whereas Geri looked damn ecstatic.

She glanced at the floor, spied a few more buttons, then raised her jubilant face back to Jeffrey. "I need to take off my coat, boots, so I'll go do that and leave you to...to..." Not finishing her thought, Geri trudged back to the front door, whistling happily.

Babette trotted behind.

Cyd looked at Jeffrey and offered a weak smile. "Caught," she whispered.

"More like catch and release." He nodded toward her chest. "One of them escaped."

"Huh?"

"Your breast..."

She looked down, releasing a weighty sigh as she nestled it back underneath the fur. "Don't know why I bother being proper considering you've seen everything."

"And it was a damn lovely everything, too," he murmured, excitement pumping through his veins as he thought of those lush breasts pressed against the glass, her breaths steaming the surface. His body had ached to taste and explore her, to take her across that hot edge of anticipation...

Then Geri and Babette had shown up and white-heat had turned stone-cold. Nothing like a mountain in a parka and a part-moose dog to put a damper on things. Probably for the best. The last thing he'd thought to pack on this trip were condoms...of course, even if he had, they'd be back in that Alpine airport.

He laughed at the craziness of it all.

"What's so funny?" asked Cyd.

"Your aunt and Babette. They're effective birth control."

Jeffrey and Cyd grinned at each other, that same lunatic smile they'd shared earlier. And in that moment, Jeffrey shared a connection with Cyd he hadn't experienced with anyone in a long, long time. A camaraderie that needed no words.

After a few moments, Cyd broke the silence. "I feel like I'm fourteen again."

"Fourteen?" He continued putting on his shirt.

"You surprised?"

He looked up, catching a funny look on Cyd's face. "Surprised?"

"That I was fourteen when I lost my virginity?"

He blinked. The conversation had taken a one-eighty and, from his past experience with women, his best resource was to wing it. Virginity. Losing it.

"I was fourteen or fifteen," he responded, checking how many buttons remained on the shirt. "That's the age, right?"

"I don't know. Never asked other girls."

Cyd pursed her lips. That had been dumb bringing up the summer she'd turned fourteen. In fact, she wasn't even sure why she had except that Jeffrey brought back memories of passion being fresh and exciting and life-changing.

But bringing up that summer resurrected other memories. Her father had had a stomach pain one month, the next he was dying. It was the summer her mom turned from a laughing, happy woman into a ghost who retreated into her room. The summer Cyd tried to fill the gaps of her family's grief, unsure what was right or wrong but wanting desperately to make her family whole again.

And it was also the summer she lost her virginity.

She didn't even remember the guy's name. Not any-more. Just that he was eighteen, house-sitting a cabin that became the only place where she could let down her guard and be herself without apology or explana-tion. Her memories were hazy, mainly recollections of long hours in dappled sunlight, the boy's body com-forting her, and her never once having to say how much life hurt.

Geri's booming voice brought Cyd out of her reverie. "I'm, uh, going into the kitchen to make coffee!" fol-lowed by heavy footsteps and the scrabbling of dog nails across the hardwood floor to the kitchen.

"I'll go with you," Cyd yelled back. "Gotta get my robe." When she caught Jeffrey's surprised look, she whispered, "She'll see it tossed over a kitchen chair so might as well warn her up-front."

"I don't think she needs to be warned...she'll be thrilled to see further evidence of our near-lusty en-counter."

Cyd grinned, nodding, glad to be back in the pres-ent, far away from that summer so long ago.

She started to scoot past Jeffrey, then stopped. Look-ing into his eyes, she fought the urge to touch the coarse hair on his cheek. Damn, the man wore rugged well.

"What're you thinking?" he asked.

That just because our sizzling encounter was prematurely interrupted, there's no reason I can't keep you indefinitely occupied in the cabin.

"Don't get dressed," she said, touching his chest.

She let her hands play a little in his hair, liking its thick, silky texture. "I'll grab my robe, a few towels, and we'll take a hot tub."

"*What?*"

"Sure! I'll tell my aunt that we're going to soak for a while—"

"No." He grabbed her hand and flashed her an are-you-crazy? look. "Even if this place had blinds on that window—" He gestured toward the glass that provided a view of the living room. "I couldn't...*soak*...with your aunt out there."

"She won't mind."

"I believe that, but that's not the point. *I* mind!"

Cyd pulled back her hand. "I'm talking *soaking*, not—"

"Whatever, I'm not getting naked in the middle of the cabin."

"Why not?"

"Because..."

Jeffrey tunneled his fingers through his hair. None of this was real. Maybe the Cessna had crash landed and this was really some drug-induced dream while he lay in a coma in a hospital bed. A grown-up version of the *Wizard of Oz*, except this would be titled *Jeffrey Amuck in Katimuk*.

He squeezed shut his eyes, hard, then reopened them.

Same snow-caked glass walls. Same bubbling hot tub. Same crazy woman naked under a pelt.

No, this was reality.

He cleared his throat. "I'm not getting naked and getting into the tub because I'd be...uncomfortable."

Cyd's mouth dropped open as though words escaped her. Oh, he should be so lucky.

"You're such a city slicker," she finally announced as though it were a newsflash.

"I prefer to be called a metropolitan man."

Cyd's mouth did that drop-open thing again. *Good.* Time to put a stopper on *that* conversation and get things back on track.

"Ask your aunt if we can borrow her snowmobile. I need to get back to the lodge, call Jordan." He continued buttoning, amazed so many were missing.

Cyd's mouth was closed again but her eyes had a funny light in them. "Uh, sure thing," she said sweetly.

Too sweetly.

He eyed her, wondering what the hell she was up to now.

"I'll go talk to her, check if we can use her snowmobile..." With an excessively disarming smile, Cyd adjusted the fur and damn near scampered off the porch and into the living room.

"Sweetie girl," Geri yelled from the kitchen, "guess what I found on my way inside! The keys to your machine. Darn things were wedged between two logs outside the front door."

Cyd skidded to a stop in front of the wood-burning stove.

Jeffrey saw her back muscles tense. "You're kidding," she said in a high-pitched voice that sounded nothing like the tough-talking Cyd he'd come to know. "Well, what a surprise!"

She sneaked a peek over her shoulder at Jeffrey, her big brown eyes saying more than any written confession.

"You hid the keys," he growled ominously. He'd skip the part about her doing that whole seduction number to distract him. Oh, she was good...

She blinked, her brown eyes glistening. And when she opened her lips to speak, he cut her off.

"Get your clothes on," Jeffrey said in a low, don't-mess-with-me tone. "And don't dawdle. In five minutes, you're driving me to the Mush Lodge."

THE RIDE TO THE LODGE WAS COLD, pushing thirty below, but that was nothing compared to the chill between Jeffrey and Cyd.

Back at the cabin, she'd gotten dressed and marched out to the snowmobile without so much as a "let's go" to Jeffrey. But he'd been ready, anticipating she'd be unrepentant. In business, he ignored people's moods and stuck to the issue.

And the issue was he needed to get to the lodge, make that call.

So when she marched outside to the snowmobile, he followed her. And although he was determined to ignore her moods, when she made a great show of huffing and puffing her indignation—releasing billowing streams of vapor into the frigid air—he had to fight the urge to smile so his teeth wouldn't freeze.

After a twenty-minute ride across the snowy wilderness to the Mush Lodge, which appeared to be all of downtown Katimuk, Cyd parked the snowmobile, cut the ignition and bounded inside without a word.

He fought the urge to be impressed at not only the longevity of her fury, but also her ability to bound in subzero weather.

When he got inside the lodge, he stamped his feet and clapped his hands in the warmth while checking out the room. The fire crackled and sputtered, one of the dogs was snoring, and scents of stew traced the air. An old Grateful Dead tune, "Truckin'," played softly in the background.

No sign of Cyd.

Jeffrey made eye contact with Charlie, who was washing glasses behind the bar. Charlie nudged his head toward the back room that housed the radio equipment. Jeffrey nodded his thanks and headed in that direction.

As he passed a group of men at the bar, conversations stopped. One or two slid him a glance.

And he thought it was freezing outside. Good thing he had Charlie on his side.

When Jeffrey entered the radio room, Cyd was perched on the wooden table, speaking into the microphone about being stranded but Mr. Bradshaw being bullheaded enough to think Jordan could work miracles. Obviously she was complaining about Jeffrey to someone at True North Airlines.

Enough was enough.

He marched up to her and took the mike. Raising it to his lips, he said authoritatively, "I don't think you understand just how serious this situation has become."

"Say again?" a man's voice responded over the radio.

Didn't sound like Jordan. Probably that red-shirted Wally fellow.

"I need, *need* to be in L.A. by the end of the day," Jeffrey said, pacing a few steps. "Do you understand that?" He paused and looked out a square window at the landscape. "There's almost two feet of snow up here, you have all my credit cards, and *I* have to get to L.A."

"I'm afraid the snow has grounded all of our flights today," the man said. "What credit cards?"

"In my coat. The pilot—" He glared at Cyd, who made a great show of turning her back to him and staring out the window as though she hadn't seen enough snow on the ride in here. "—put me in some kind of giant parka but then left *my* coat behind. What kind of an outfit is this?"

"The parka's a necessity in the Cessna. And, I can assure you, your credit cards are perfectly safe," the man said evenly. "And, I understand your frustration. I truly wish I had an easy solution."

All this smooth talking was getting Jeffrey nowhere. "And, I truly wish you understood the problem!"

"So, why don't you explain it to me?" the man said politely.

Good God Almighty. These people needed to light fires under their *ambitions*, not just in their stoves. "I have an important meeting in L.A. at eleven o'clock

Monday morning," he said, enunciating each word so the importance of his goal would sink in. "If I'm not at that meeting, I will lose my promotion, and most certainly lose the Alaska television series."

"There's going to be a television series in Alaska?"

"Not if I stay stuck in Katimuk with the pilot from hell, there's not."

Cyd crossed her arms and emitted a long-suffering sigh.

"What kind of a television series?" the man asked.

This Wally-guy's questions were taking up precious time. "It would have been called *Sixty Below,* a comedy about the lives and loves of the people in Arctic Luck," said Jeffrey tightly. "Would. Note the word *would.* I never did get to Arctic Luck, strike one. I can't take pictures of anything in the blizzard, strike two. And I can't get to the pitch meeting tomorrow, strike three."

"Can't you pitch it by phone?" asked the man, sounding so polite and concerned, Jeffrey's irritation level kicked up twofold.

"Pitch what?" he barked. "I've never even *seen* the town. And, no, it's not something you do by phone. I need pictures, drawings, storyboards." God, how did these people survive day-to-day?

"Of Arctic Luck."

"No. Of San Diego. Of course of Arctic Luck."

"If...uh...somebody else went to the meeting, with pictures and diagrams, could you tell them what to say?"

"Won't work," snapped Jeffrey, shooting a look at

Cyd, who had suddenly taken an interest in her finger-nails. Yeah, right. She cared about fingernails like other women cared about nosediving Cessnas.

"Why not?" asked the man over the radio.

"They won't take the pitch from anybody but me."

Jeffrey leaned against the table, fighting the sinking sensation that no matter what he asked for, what he demanded, he might as well beat his head against the log wall. His career was destroyed.

"What if it was you?" asked the man.

Maybe things weren't that glum. Jeffrey straightened. "You're sending a flight?"

"No. I'm sending Jordan."

Jeffrey froze. "Jordan?"

"My boss," said the man. "The guy who looks just like you."

"Jordan's flying up here?"

"Nope. We send Jordan to L.A."

"What?" Jeffrey swore he heard an echo on the other end of the radiophone. Another man's voice exclaiming the same thing.

"Holy cow," said Wally. "Even your voices sound the same."

"I'm not going to L.A.," said the man in the background.

Now *that* was Jordan. The one Jeffrey recalled seeing through that window at the Alpine Airport. "That's ridiculous," Jeffrey said, imagining that rustic look-alike trying to pass himself off as Jeffrey. No way.

"He looks just like you," said Wally.

The static crackled on the radio.

Jeffrey shook his head. "It's not—"

"He does," blurted Cyd, who immediately pursed her lips as though she wished she hadn't said it.

Jeffrey glared at her, then at the mike as though he might see through the metal, down the wires, into that cramped airport at Jordan. He recalled the wild, curling hair over the collar. The tan, weathered face. The clothes straight out of *Nanook of the North.* No, no way in hell. They'd have an easier time trying to pass off Clousseau for James Bond.

"Sure," said Jordan in the background, in an oh-so-cool voice. "Anything for customer satisfaction."

Was Jordan crazy?

"We give him a haircut," said Wally over the radio. "You tell Jordan exactly what to say. He goes to the meeting, then flies back home."

Obviously more than the water froze up here during these snow squalls. People's brains froze, too. "Never in a million years," said Jeffrey. End of discussion.

"You got a better idea?" asked Wally.

"Fly up here and get me," demanded Jeffrey.

"No can do. Tell me, what's the worst that would happen if Jordan tried and failed?"

"The series is dumped, and my career is ruined."

"What will happen if you don't make the meeting?"

"The series gets dumped, and my career is ruined."

"What are the odds of success?"

Jeffrey paused. "Ten percent."

"That's ten percent better than we've got going for us now."

Maybe not everyone's brains were frozen. This

Wally fellow was starting to make sense. Jeffrey stared out at the frozen landscape, realizing this far-fetched idea of being represented in L.A. might not be so far-fetched, after all. Ten percent was better than zero.

"We have pictures of Arctic Luck," said Wally.

"Good ones?" asked Jeffrey.

"*Great* ones."

Compelling photos of the setting for *Sixty Below*. And no one had seen Jeffrey in the past year...wasn't so strange if he'd bulked up a bit, had maybe spent more time outdoors. A vacation or two in the Caribbean would explain the tan. And looking weathered? Hell, he was an executive. Back-to-back meetings could give anyone a more weathered look.

He imagined Jordan with a haircut, in a suit, coached on exactly what to say. All he had to do was fake it for one meeting. And if anyone asked questions about Alaska—the weather, the people, the facilities—who better than Jordan to field such questions?

"First thing he needs to know is the org chart," said Jeffrey, pacing a few feet, feeling that familiar rush of adrenaline that said success was within reach. Oh, yeah, this could work. "There's a copy of last year's annual report in the right hand, top drawer of the desk in my condo. Keys to the condo are in my coat pocket..."

He grinned to himself as he rattled off more instructions into the mike, ignoring Cyd's sullen you-aren't-getting-away-with-this stare.

The little actress was going to have to learn a new role.

6

JEFFREY BLINKED OPEN HIS EYES, lulled awake by the scent of strong coffee. Spying the braided rug on the floor, he idly wondered who had replaced the Persian when a woman's voice belted, "Good morning, Jeff!"

He raised his head and focused blearily on the mass blocking light from the far window. Slowly his eyes adjusted and he recognized Geri's blue gray flannel shirt. He followed the line of her long silver braid up to her round face, toothy grin and the expectant gleam in her eyes.

Man, she was too much morning for him.

"Morning, Ger," he said with a yawn. The crackling fire in the wood-burning stove blended with the distant sputtering of frying bacon.

"Storm hit last night," Geri said in a booming voice. "Got another four feet of snow."

He squinted past her at the window, which offered the picture of a vast, frigid world.

Hell, that's nothing compared to the freeze between Cyd and I.

They hadn't spoken since yesterday's "key mystery" was solved. Well, a few words during his call with Jordan, but those didn't really count as interpersonal communication. No, his and Cyd's communication had mostly been a long chilly silence that continued all the way through last night's meal. If Geri hadn't talked about the time Cyd had dissected a buffalo on a high school biology trip, there would've been zero dinner conversation.

"Sleep well?" Geri asked.

"Uh, hmm." Best he had in weeks, actually. But then, who wouldn't have been bone-tired after the last forty-eight hours. Long hours of travel via plane, dog team and snowmobile. Add the energy-draining crises of losing luggage and almost losing his TV series and even Superman would have felt fatigued.

But the most trying element had to be Cyd. Yesterday he'd thought of her as a tornado. Last night he'd upgraded that to a hurricane. Miraculously he'd been able to not only weather her storms, but subdue them. Temporarily, anyway.

He wasn't worried about the little snow squall outside. His concern was what was next in the Cyd forecast.

Geri stepped forward and said softly, "She's a great girl, ya know."

She undoubtedly wanted to address the obvious tension she'd been witnessing between he and Cyd. He didn't want to go there, however. Not until he had a cup of coffee. Or a martini. Double.

Geri took a step toward him and he sensed her eagerness to continue this Cyd conversation.

"Yes, she's, uh, great," he mumbled, not adding that Cyd might be a good girl, but she was also a very pissed-off one, too, for some reason tied to the TV series. And it sure would be nice to know that reason so his stay in Katimuk didn't disintegrate into a prison sentence with tough girl-guard Cyd.

"Her father—Buddy—was my kid brother," Geri said, gesturing with the spatula. "Cyd was the apple of his eye, his daddy's girl."

Maybe if he understood more of Cyd's past, he might understand some of her present, too. Like why she disliked his business goals so much. Why she was a thorn in his progress for the series, for his promotion.

"Tell me more," he prompted.

Geri stopped in front of the fire. Golden light flickered over her face as she stared at the family picture on the wall, the same photo he'd looked at night before last. In his mind's eye, he could still see a fourteen-year-old Cyd, gangly and sweet-faced with her hair falling prettily to her shoulders.

Geri talked while staring at the photo. "Buddy had barely moved here before he got sick. We lost him fast, within two months." She shook her head slowly, as though the comprehension was still unfathomable. "Cyd changed fast after that, too. Went from little girl to woman in the blink of an eye. Had no choice, I guess, with her mother retreating into her grief. The younger kids needed someone to take care of them..."

Geri returned her gaze to Jeffrey, and he caught the shimmer of emotion in her eyes. "I tried to help, but lived too far away to travel that often. When I could, though, I showed Cyd how to cook, hunt. Never forget seeing that wisp of a girl bag her first moose. It not only fed her family, but several of the neighbors as well, for months." Geri smiled, shaking her head. Obviously, the older woman was still impressed with her niece's feat.

Geri bent down and moved one of Babette's toys, a plastic mouse missing an ear. "A year later, her mom was more herself but Cyd seemed afraid to stop being the family caretaker. As though if she let go, everything would fall apart."

Jeffrey thought of Cyd swaggering into the Alpine Airport with the attitude of someone three times her size. All bluster and know-it-all.

"By the time she was sixteen," Geri continued, tossing the doggie toy out of the way of foot traffic, "she'd chopped off her hair and was learning to fly an old DeHavilland. She was helping out some local pilots—doing some minor mechanics and helping stock flights—which earned her money. I don't know what her mom and siblings would have done without Cyd's grit. She not only brought home a paycheck, but also hunted, trapped. She's great at those things, but her siblings are picking up the slack these days. Plus her mother has a decent job. Cyd's mentioned going back to school, studying engineering, but she'll never do that until she lets go of that 'I'm the head of the family' role."

"She's still wearing her father's shoes," Jeffrey murmured.

"Yeah, that's right. Never accepts help from anyone else, either. Just like her father."

Like father, like daughter. The pieces of the family puzzle were forming a picture in Jeffrey's mind, albeit a hazy one. "So that photo was taken the summer her family moved to Alaska, the summer her father..."

"Died. Yes."

"What kind of work did he do?"

"Odd jobs. Some mining, carpentry until he could get his feet back on the ground."

"No, before Alaska."

"Oh." Geri paused. "He ran the fanciest movie house in Seattle. You shoulda seen it."

He hadn't heard this tone in Geri's voice before. Almost reverential. It was funny to hear this big, robust woman wax poetic over something.

She waved her spatula around the room. "Walls were painted with images of Egypt—pharaohs, pyramids, camels. The theater had big seats, covered in a red velvetlike fabric. And right before the movie began—" Geri raised a hand slowly, waggling her fingers "—a shimmering gold curtain raised in rich, thick folds to reveal the screen." Geri's eyes glistened as she stared off into the distance.

She dropped her hand and sighed. "It was magnificent, I tell ya. Downright magical. And Cyd was always there, doing everything from working the concession stand to threading the film. I swore that little girl would grow up to be a movie star the way she lived and breathed films."

He stared, wordlessly. *This* was news. Cyd, starry-eyed over images on the silver screen? He'd imagined her growing up idolizing Amelia Earhart, not Julia Roberts. "What happened to the theater?" *What happened to Cyd?*

Geri shook her head sadly. "One of those big chain of movie theaters moved into that section of Seattle. They offered everything from video games in the lobby to more movies to bigger screens. Buddy couldn't compete. He toyed with turning the theater into a film art house—you know, those movies with words at the bottom of the screen—but there wasn't enough interest. He sold the building to a real estate agent who razed it and built a parking lot."

"A parking lot," Jeffrey repeated, imaging an ugly patch of black asphalt replacing a majestic piece of yesterday. Sadly enough, whoever owned that property probably made more money parking cars than the old, outdated theater would have made. "Did...the father live to see that?"

"Thank God, no. Cyd visited a girlfriend during that time and saw the parking lot, but she never talked about it."

"That had been her dream world," Jeffrey said under his breath. He'd never known such a spot himself growing up, except in books. As an adult, he created spots that were akin to dream worlds. Refuges, really. His loft in New York. His home in L.A. Places he could escape to, surround himself with things he loved.

But those were contrived comforts that couldn't compare to what Cyd had experienced growing up in that theater. A place of family and dreams. He envied her. He'd always lived through imaginary worlds in books, but she'd lived the real thing.

Geri crossed to the picture and adjusted it. "Buddy so loved that theater..."

Jeffrey let his mind wander, wondering what had happened after the family lost the theater. Why had the father chosen Alaska, a place so far removed from things like golden curtains and movie stars? Just as confusing was Cyd's change of heart. *If she loved movies, why try so hard to stop my series?*

A form stumbled in from the hallway. A sleepy-faced Cyd, her body dwarfed in that oversize red-and-gray robe, shuffled in. At first he thought she was wearing shapeless slippers, then realized they were stretched-out argyle socks.

He stared at the robe, recalling what lay underneath—the supple skin, tight curves, lush breasts. Most women he knew flaunted their bodies in revealing, plunging clothes. Idly he wondered how Cyd would look if she ever dared to try on a feminine look.

"Mornin', Aunt Geri." Cyd yawned, ruffling her fingers through her spiky black hair.

Geri wrapped a welcoming arm around her niece. "Mornin', sweetie girl. Why don't ya keep our guest company while I finish cooking breakfast."

Cyd slid a peeved glance at Jeffrey.

"Morning," he said.

She muttered something that sounded like "mornin'" but he couldn't be sure.

Geri headed for the kitchen, then stopped and turned back to them. "I got a problem with the oilstove in the basement. Carburetor needs adjusting. Looks like the valve slipped again, and now crud is clogging the pipes, dripping on the unit."

"I'll fix it," Cyd said, stretching her bare arms toward the fire.

"It's a lot of work," said Geri, her voice trailing off.

Cyd's chin angled up. "I'll take care of it. Right after breakfast."

Jeffrey caught Geri's look. Her eyes were glistening with an unasked question.

Oh, no, no, no. She wanted him to volunteer to help Cyd, which he didn't mind doing, but *not* for the reasons Geri wanted. Hell, did all Alaskan women practice the fine art of matchmaking with a sledgehammer? First Geri encouraged Jeffrey and Cyd to romp naked in a hot tub, now to go into the basement and co-fix an oilstove.

Geri still pinned him with a look, which had taken on a pleading quality.

Oh, hell, he owed it to his host to help out...as long as she didn't push the romance angle. Anyway, this was a golden opportunity to talk with Cyd, get her to open up. Maybe he'd hit on a topic that would reveal what, exactly, bothered her about his TV series. If he knew the issue, he could resolve it. It would be a lot easier to have Cyd on his side these next few days considering she was his taxi service to and from the lodge.

"I'll help," Jeffrey chimed in.

Cyd shot him a furious look. "*I* can do it. I don't need—"

"Wonderful!" Geri said, her booming voice drowning out her niece's. "We'll eat breakfast, then you two can fix the stove."

A FEW HOURS LATER, CYD flicked off her flashlight and tossed it into the metal toolbox. On a release of breath, she stared at the stove. It was a hardworking beauty, a curvaceous body of cast iron and nickel that—thanks to Cyd's and Jeffrey's cleaning—now gleamed again with a stately air.

She touched the valve again, ensuring it was securely set.

"It would take some effort to reset this valve," she muttered, giving it a little wiggle. When Cyd had first checked out the stove, the valve had been turned a good ninety degrees off from its normal setting. The additional oil into the carburetor threw off its adjustment causing fluid to clog the pipes and seep over the unit.

But now that she tested it multiple times, seeing if it slipped easily, it didn't. "Maybe Babette nudged it when she brushed past..."

Not like Geri, though, to let Babette romp around this piece of equipment. The stove provided valuable heat to the cabin. It'd be foolish for her aunt to chance any condition, such as a dog on the loose, that might make the heating stove inoperable.

On the other hand, Geri might not have known Babette had been down there. The dog was a wily character. If you left a door open, she went for it. The glassed-in porch, for example. How many times had Babette played chew toy with the plastic covering on the tub...or played doggie-nymphette in the tub itself?

I'll remind Geri to double-check that the door leading to the basement is locked at all times.

Cyd withdrew her fingers from the valve and shifted

her gaze to Jeffrey. He was holding his flashlight on one of the nickel-cast legs where he industriously wiped off a streak of oil. The only other light down here was a single overhead bulb that glossed the room in a hazy yellow light.

She watched Jeffrey as he sat back on his heels and scoured the section of the stove he'd just worked on. Was he this detailed in life as well? Focusing on minutiae, getting it exactly right? She flashed on a distant memory of her father renovating a section of wall painting—a pharaoh sitting majestically on a throne—at the movie theater. A ten-year-old Cyd had tiptoed around, not wanting to disturb her father's concentration. And when the repainting had been completed, she'd not only been awed at the result, but ever after, linked the man on the throne with her father.

She clenched her jaw, refusing to give into emotion. *Don't link Jeffrey to a noble image. He's here to destroy your world, not protect it.*

Wally could have the True North Airlines' employee-of-the-month bonus because when Cyd got a chance, she was going to tell it like it was to Jordan. Tell him he'd gone over the edge with this customer-relationship fixation. That flying to L.A. to appease one citified guy for—gasp—being weathered in wasn't customer relations. It was aiding and abetting the enemy!

Today the enemy wanted yet another of those calls with Jordan. Something about squeezing in some last-minute "coaching" before Jordan attended some mucky-muck meeting. All last night lying in bed, Cyd had plotted ways to sabotage the radiophone and make it unusable...a fantasy only because in reality, the community needed that radio.

Interesting, though, how Jeffrey seemed oblivious to her black mood. All through their stove cleaning, he'd acted as though her cold front were just as warm as could be, even asking her chitchatty questions about what had it been like growing up here in Alaska, what did she like best about her life, what did she do for "fun."

Even in school she hadn't had such dumb conversations with girlfriends.

So she'd refused to answer and stayed focused on cleaning the stove.

Cyd picked up a few of the soiled rags while checking out Jeffrey. The yellow light burnished the tips of his hair, giving him a dark angel effect. When he leaned a certain way, light slanted across his face, highlighting the strong line of his nose, the firm curve of his mouth.

A flame of heat licked her insides.

Dammit, anyway. It pissed her off to be attracted to him. She reminded herself it wasn't weakness, just biological instinct causing this reaction. *After all, I'm flesh and blood, not steel.* And it had been a while since she'd been with a man *that way.* Months, in fact. She was just overdue and Jeffrey happened to be here.

Nothing weak about that.

But that feeling was more than biological instinct. To be honest, she'd felt a grudging respect for the guy when he showed up in the basement wearing jeans and a flannel shirt—some of Calvin's clothes Geri had loaned Jeffrey—rolling up his sleeves to get to work. It was as though he'd shed the sophisticated city boy and evolved into a rugged Alaskan.

Yeah, okay, that explained her attraction. She saw the Alaskan in him, that's all. Couldn't blame a girl for being drawn to her own kind.

He dropped his flashlight into the toolbox and looked at her. "You finished?"

"Yes. Just triple-checked the valve. Everything's fine." Up to now, she'd muttered a few thoughts to herself, but this was the first time she'd actually *conversed* with Jeffrey in almost twenty-four hours. Was that a slight smile curving his lips?

"We're a good team," he said.

Don't push your luck, city man. "You through?" she snapped.

He did a last swipe of the rag on a curve of finial. "Yes," he answered politely, tossing the rag into the bag with the other dirty ones. Blowing out a gust of breath, he swiped his hand across his forehead which left a streak of oil.

"You need to be careful—" She stopped.

"What?"

Ah-ha! An idea sparkled in her mind. She didn't have to sabotage the radiophone...she just had to sabotage Jeffrey *getting* to it again.

"Sorry I've been so quiet," she said, putting some oozy niceness in her voice.

Even in the muted light, she saw him flinch. Okay, she'd cool the sweet-voiced stuff. Didn't want to inadvertently alert the enemy she was planning a maneuver.

"Yes," he said slowly, "you've been...quiet." Even in the feeble light, she saw how his eyes bored into her, trying to fathom her game.

Cyd had the sense they were playing chess again. Watching each other's moves while planning their next one.

"I was pissed at you," she said brusquely. Yeah, that was good—she was talking like the Cyd he expected. Tough, to the point.

His shoulders relaxed a little. "Because?" he asked.

"Because...I didn't like Jordan flying to L.A." Well, that was the truth. Sort of. Didn't want to spill everything, like how she was willing to do almost anything to get Jeffrey and his big business out of her state, forever.

"He's doing me a favor."

"I've, uh, come to realize that," she said. "He's sacrificing his duties as president of True North Airlines for the greater good." Hey, she was sounding pretty convincing at this heartfelt stuff. Plus, it sounded like a perfectly plausible excuse for her irked behavior. Maybe Jeffrey wasn't so far off base with that actress comment. Of course, she'd grown up watching more movies than most kids—maybe she did have some natural acting ability.

She caught a glint in Jeffrey's eyes. *He's buying it.* Good. If he thinks this is more about my wanting Jordan back here, he won't be anticipating my next plan of attack.

"You and Jordan are...close?"

"Close?" She paused. "You think we're..." *Jordan?* He was a nice guy, a fair boss, but she and Jordan, *romantic?* She started to quip something about their only relations being customer relations when a thought zapped her.

Oh, yeah, I can use this.

Cyd sighed dramatically, the way she'd seen Meryl Streep do in *Postcards from the Edge.* "Oh...that was a long time ago." Cyd blinked her eyes rapidly as though struggling with some heart-wrenching angst. Then she reached over and stroked her fingers lightly down the right side of Jeffrey's face, her fingers tingling over the emerging beard. "How kind of you to care."

He made a grunting noise, possibly of disbelief, but he didn't move. The man was still her captive audience. Her fingers reached his chin, which she gave a little squeeze with her forefinger and thumb. After one more heartfelt sigh, she pulled her hand away, admiring her work.

Half of his face was streaked with black soot, the dark blotch on his chin reminiscent of a goatee.

"So..." Jeffrey said, drawing out the word. "You don't like the idea of a TV series because you think he'll be involved somehow?"

"He'll?"

"Jordan."

"Oh, right." *Stay focused!* "Right, he'll be involved and I won't see him as much." She moved a little so the light from the bulb hit her face. Like an actress under a spotlight, she smiled bravely. "I know I should move on, but it's been hard. There are other men, sure, but you saw the pickings at the lodge."

Jeffrey nodded a bit too readily.

Cyd fought the urge to roll her eyes. "But I need to move on, put the past behind me," she whispered, cupping her other hand to the left side of Jeffrey's face. "Knowing you has made that difficult. You look like him, you know." She patted his cheek before dropping her hand.

Excellent. Jeffrey looked like the Prince of Darkness with all that soot and crud on his face. She'd just made a killer move in this chess game. Bye-bye TV series.

"Let's go upstairs," she said sweetly, "and tell Geri her stove is as good as new. I'll bring the toolbox, you grab the rags."

A few minutes later, they headed up the stairs to the kitchen where Geri was stirring something in a bowl. The scent of vanilla threaded the air. Babette was chewing on his plastic mouse, which emitted occasional squeaks.

"All done!" Cyd called out.

"Great, sweetie girl—" Geri turned and froze. "Jeff...what'd you do? Clean the stove with your face?"

"What?"

Geri set down her bowl and held up the silver toaster. "Look at yourself."

He squinted, blinked, and muttered an expletive. Then he turned and leveled a look at Cyd. "You," he said, pointing a finger at her. "I *knew* you were up to something. What, I still don't know."

Cyd blinked, doing her best to maintain a *who-me-what?* look. Feigning a double take at his face, she looked at her dirty hands and gasped as though seeing them for the first time. "I had no idea—"

"What happened down there?" asked Geri, setting down the toaster.

"She rubbed her filthy hands all over my face," Jeffrey said tightly. "No, didn't just rub. Squeezed, stroked..."

"Oh good!" blurted Geri.

Jeffrey and Cyd both turned and looked at Geri, whose face flamed pink. "I mean, good that you're...talking again. Listen, the shower is still under construction, so you can't wash up there. And I'd suggest washing up in the bathroom sink, but I don't want all my towels getting gunked up with oil and soot."

Cyd fought the urge to smile at her aunt's conniving ways. That little "oh good" was as good as a confession. So Aunt Geri cranked the valve out of position to get Cyd and Jeffrey into some "cozy" situation. If the entire scenario hadn't played into a perfect plan for Cyd, she'd be telling her aunt to chill the matchmaking right now.

But instead, the oilstove scenario had provided inspiration for Cyd. She'd purposefully "dirtied" Jeffrey up, knowing Geri would balk at his using precious water and smearing oil all over her towels. This was the moment Cyd had been waiting for.

"No problem," she said sweetly. "Weather's temporarily cleared. Jeffrey and I can easily scoot over to the Suds and Showers."

"Perfect!" Geri agreed, picking up the bowl and stirring again.

"Suds and Showers?" Jeffrey said, his eyes growing darker than the soot on his face.

"It's a washeteria nearby," explained Cyd, "where people pay to use the shower, washing machine and other facilities."

He glanced at the wall clock. "No time. It's almost 10:15. 9:15 in L.A. The sooner I call, the better chance of catching Jordan before the meeting. Trust me, he won't care if I have some oil on my face. I could be tarred and feathered for all he knows."

"Oh, but Charlie wouldn't be too happy if you cart crud into the lodge," said Cyd. "Anyway, Suds and Showers is on the way. If we leave now, you'll be washed up, in clean clothes and at the Mush in, oh, forty minutes tops."

Jeffrey cocked an eyebrow. "Really?"

"Really."

"And there's no problem with the snowmobile or the keys? I don't want to be stuck in the middle of nowhere."

Cyd made a dismissive gesture. "There's no way I'd ever endanger our lives by stranding us outside in this weather. I know yesterday I hid the keys—I admit that—but I was upset about Jordan. I'm better now." If she kept smiling like this, she was going to pull a muscle in her face.

Jeffrey looked at her through slitted eyes. "Why are you suddenly helping me so much?"

"Just like I told you, I now realize that the more I help, the sooner Jordan can get back home and run True North Airlines. We need him here, you know." Actually, Wally was a great fill-in for Jordan, had overseen the business numerous times when Jordan took a vacation, but who cared about such facts at a time like this?

She stepped closer, catching Jeffrey's masculine scent. It swirled through her head, igniting heated thoughts. *Stay focused.* "Sorry," she whispered.

"For what?" he asked. His sullen look was growing confused again.

Oh, I'm good. "For my having been so difficult." She debated whether to bat her eyes a time or two, but figured it would be overkill.

Jeffrey searched her eyes. "We better get going, then," he murmured.

"You're absolutely right." Jeffrey would never hear *those* words again from the lips of Cyd Thompson.

"I'll, uh, go get you two some clean clothes to take with you," said Geri, setting down the bowl on the counter. "Calvin's seem to fit you just fine, Jeff." As she exited the kitchen, Babette trotted after her, the dog's toenails clicking on the linoleum floor.

Cyd and Jeffrey held each other's gaze for several long, drawn out moments. The scent of vanilla still teased the air, triggering memories of yesterday. In Cyd's mind, she saw Jeffrey storming onto the glassed-in deck, ripping off his shirt. And she wondered if he was recalling the same thing because his eyes burned brighter, simmering with hidden fires.

"What are you up to, Cyd?" he whispered huskily, leaning his head toward hers. He arched one eyebrow, teasing and challenging her at the same time.

It was all she could do to stare up into his face. A face coarse with stubble, smeared with soot like some kind of Navy Seal on a dangerous mission. His raw sexuality was doing wicked things to her insides. She suppressed the urge to shudder, determined to show him she didn't buckle under his roughened city charm.

"Nothing," she whispered, tilting up her chin.

Big mistake.

It notched her lips closer to his. So close, she could feel hot puffs of his breath against her mouth, triggering wild fantasies of what it would be like to kiss him, taste him.

She slicked a tongue over her bottom lip. "We should go," she whispered shakily, wanting to stay strong. In control.

Knowing damn well she'd just lost a move in this chess game.

7

THE SNOWMOBILE JERKED to a stop in front of a log cabin on whose front door was painted Suds And Showers in bright yellow. Cyd cut the motor and started to get off, then cast a look over her shoulder at Jeffrey.

"You can let go," she said, her voice muffled behind the frost-caked ski mask.

"I'm trying," Jeffrey muffled back, wondering if his lips had merged with his wool mask. Plus, his arms had been encircled around her waist for so long, his sleeves were frozen stiff.

With great effort, he released his grip and got off the machine. Then he crunched across the powdered snow, almost getting teary-eyed at the scent of coffee and cooking meat wafting from the cabin.

Me, the guy who loves tofu, is getting emotional over meat.

He trudged up the snow-laden steps to the porch, not wanting to further contemplate that last thought. It took enough concentration and effort to put one foot in front of the other in this world turned walk-in freezer.

He shoved open the heavy wooden door and stepped into a small living room crowded with chairs, several coatracks, stacks of books and games. He tugged off his ski mask and breathed deeply, staring across the room at a blazing fire, near which lay two bear-sized dogs. One raised its massive black head, sniffed, then lay back down.

Don't blame you, buddy. I wouldn't be interested in a walking icicle, either.

Heavy footsteps followed Jeffrey inside. He turned and watched Cyd stomping her feet on the welcome mat. After tossing aside a plastic sack filled with the clean clothes Geri had packed for them, Cyd pulled off her mittens. Then she tugged off her ski mask, unveiling her flushed cheeks, sparkling eyes, and untamed hair.

An odd shiver that had nothing to do with the cold raced over his skin. Damn, she looked beautiful.

Noting how the room's hazy glow caressed the curve of her cheekbone and warmed her eyes to a velvety brown, something in his chest constricted. An indefinable ache that took him by surprise. And he had the sudden, crazy idea that this woman held the answer to something he'd been seeking for a long time.

He tore his gaze off her and began unlacing a boot. Crazy idea, all right. Cyd and her moods had provided more questions than answers. No, he took that back. He had *one* answer. He finally understood that she'd been uptight about the TV series because she blamed it for Jordan's absence. But other things still didn't make sense. Like why a woman who didn't mince words would resort to such bizarre nonverbal techniques as sooting up his face.

Not that he could always figure women out, but Cyd was definitely in a league all her own.

"Judy? Jerry?" Cyd called out, working off one of her boots. When there was no answer, she lowered her voice, "If they were here, their dogs would be, too. They're probably picking up supplies."

He looked questioningly at the dogs by the fire.

"Not those dogs," Cyd explained. "The sled dogs."

She tossed aside her boots and dug into a pile of socks and slippers kept in a basket next to the front door. After putting on a pair of knitted slip-ons, Cyd shuffled toward a doorway to their right. "Let's grab some coffee while we're getting undressed."

While we're getting undressed?

He watched her walk away, that compact rear end undulating in a pair of snug jeans, and wondered if she'd return naked. After all, Cyd did seem to get overly aroused in kitchens. He tugged off his other boot, thinking how for the rest of his life, the scent of vanilla would be an aphrodisiac to him.

As he retrieved a pair of socks from the basket and put them on, Cyd reentered the living room with two steaming mugs of coffee. Stopping before him, she offered him one. "You don't take sugar, right?"

"No, just vanilla."

"What?"

"No, I don't take sugar." *Shouldn't have thought about yesterday's vanilla incident.* Accepting the coffee, he glanced out the window at the frozen world, willing some of that cold into his heated thoughts.

Didn't work.

All that white looked like an endless panorama of sheets and pillows upon which he imagined Cyd's body stretched, her dark head thrashing as she arched in ecstasy underneath him.

He slugged back a mouthful of hot java. *Cool it with the kitchen vanilla scents and snow-as-bed fantasies. And while you're at it, cool it with the moose meat fantasies, too.*

Jeffrey had more than his share of street savvy, but as he'd grown more successful in the business world, he'd also grown more polished, cultured. But that seemed to slip away up here. As though the call of the wild permeated a man's being, seeping through his skin and bones until it altered the very formation of his DNA. If Jeffrey didn't watch it, next he'd insist on being called Wolf and take a job hawking moose jerky along the Denali Highway.

"Jeffrey?"

Pop. Back to reality. "Yes?"

"You okay?"

No. "Yes."

"You were looking...odd for a moment there." Cyd set her coffee on the window ledge and began removing her parka. "Hungry? Smells like Judy is roasting some caribou."

"God, no." When the series got up here, he'd insist the catering crew stock some normal fare. Veggie burgers. An espresso machine. Several juicers. That should stave off any DNA alterations.

"All right," Cyd said, looking at him as though she wasn't sure if he was or not. "Let's do showers. Fortunately there isn't a line of people waiting. Once I waited almost two hours!"

She hung her parka on a peg. "When Judy or Jerry

aren't here, it's an honor system." Cyd gestured to a nearby oak table, on top of which was a metal box. In front of it was sign on which was scrawled Showers, $5. Washing Machine, $4. Dryer, $3.

"My wallet's back in Alpine." Jeffrey thought a moment. "No, make that L.A.," he said glumly. "Jordan has it."

"Too bad," Cyd quipped. "No money, no shower!" She picked up her coffee and took a sip. "But because I accidentally got your face all dirty, my treat."

Accident, my ass, thought Jeffrey.

He removed his parka rather than further ponder the mysteries of Cyd. Besides, now that the subject of Jordan had come up, Jeffrey needed to focus on cleaning up, getting to the lodge, making his call.

He'd start out reviewing Jordan on the basics. Then review the org charts, bring him up to speed on Argonaut's key players. He'd remind Jordan who to trust—namely, Jeffrey's best pal Rob—and who to never turn his back on—foremost being Jeffrey's nemesis, Ashley Baines.

"Mind if I go first?" Cyd asked, heading toward the fire. She stepped over the dogs and edged close to the grating.

"Ladies first." Jeffrey hung up his parka.

"You're in Alaska, city boy, not Paris."

"Right," he said, "where men are men and women are…" His mind turned into Swiss cheese as she peeled off her navy blue sweater.

No bra.

Cyd's skin glowed golden and crimson in the flickering firelight. A golden haze caught in her curves, emphasizing the womanliness in that taut, compact body.

"Women are what?" Cyd dropped the sweater on to the ground.

"Beautiful," he murmured. "One woman in particular."

Cyd stood, her hands poised on her jeans zipper, an embarrassed blush staining her cheeks. If he wasn't mistaken, he saw a flash of panic in her eyes. Instinctively he knew what was going on with her. His murmured compliment had shaken her up, and if there's anything Cyd Thompson didn't like, it was losing her equilibrium, being out of control. Oh, she didn't mind doing things to make *him* out of control, but the lady didn't like the tables turned.

As though she read his thoughts, she suddenly unzipped her jeans and, with great gusto, whipped them off. He'd never seen a woman so flustered trying to get undressed.

Grabbing the waistband of her white cotton undies, she leaned over to pull them down and he wished time would freeze.

Because in that position, her breasts hung like fruit, ripe for the picking...and nibbling and sucking. And the way her thumbs tucked in the waistband, pulling out the underwear just a little, he had a mouthwatering glimpse of tight black curls.

"What're you looking at?" she snapped.

He looked up to see Cyd's blazing black eyes looking at him.

"I'm looking at even more beautiful," he answered huskily.

Damn if her cheeks didn't flame redder.

As though to prove she still had the upper hand, she yanked down the underwear and scooped them up with the rest of her clothes. Straightening, she leveled him a look he was sure was meant to show him who's boss. If she only knew that getting such a fired-up, dare-you look from a naked woman—well, the armful of clothes covered her breasts, but the rest was still deliciously exposed—was about the most titillating moment he'd ever experienced.

"Instead of staring at something you've seen before," she said, "why don't you get out of your wet clothes?"

She didn't quite sound herself. A little breathy. A lot out of control.

"I'm getting to you, aren't I?" he said, not breaking their eye lock.

"No."

"Like hell."

Her eyes darkened with emotion and he swore he saw the clothes jiggle a little. Was she shaking?

He had to bite his inner cheek to not smile. She might be a little actress, but she wasn't pulling off this I-don't-feel-anything role very well.

He wondered how long she'd stand there, butt naked, playing stare-down. It was warmer near the fire, which was undoubtedly why she'd stripped over there, but not warm enough to stay there much longer with nothing between her and God but a layer of very pretty skin.

"Well, if I'm not getting to you, why are the clothes quivering?"

She raised her chin a notch. "I—I—I—"

Shivering, are we?

With an indignant huff, Cyd turned and strode toward the other doorway, which had to lead to the shower. If he thought that bottom undulated nicely in jeans—naked was an even better story.

Without looking back, Cyd announced, "There's baskets outside the shower for dirty clothes. When it's your turn, toss your old clothes in with mine. We'll leave them here to be washed and dried."

He watched her straight-backed body disappear into the shadowed hallway, knowing she was doing her damnedest to leave a last impression that no matter what had just transpired, Mr. Jeffrey Bradshaw didn't have *that* much effect on her.

One of the dogs raised its nose and snorted.

"I know, buddy. She likes me."

Jeffrey scrubbed a hand across his face. Just as her act didn't disguise her feelings, he couldn't disguise his, either. He liked her, too. Liked her gutsy, this-is-how-I-am attitude. She was fiery and fearless. He knew women who behaved that way in the business world, but God help them if they were plunked down here in the middle of the Alaskan interior. Cyd would run circles around them.

He chuckled, imaging some citified woman complaining about a broken fingernail. Cyd wouldn't complain if she broke her whole damn arm. Not a crack in that armor, no sir.

But his admiration turned to a moment of sadness when he thought of that young girl who spent dreamy hours in her father's movie theater. He'd bet she didn't wear her armor then. Just as the theater had been torn down and paved over, had she covered that little girl's starry-eyed vision with the toughened woman's no-nonsense one?

As the rush of water started down the hall, he released the thought and wandered around the living room perusing the piles of books. A few mysteries by Dashiell Hammett, Agatha Christie. A stack of tattered science fiction paperbacks. He checked out the back cover of one he'd read when he was fifteen, a sci-fi novel starring a family called Lies. He'd related to it because nothing seemed real in his own life, living with a series of families who were strangers.

He became aware of a radio playing softly. He'd probably missed it in the noisy commotion of his and Cyd's arrival and subsequent tête à tête. Straining to hear the tune, he belatedly realized it was Cyd singing. In a soft, honeyed voice she hummed fragments from an old Springsteen song, one of the boss's slower, moodier numbers where he got down and dirty about the complexities of love.

Jeffrey glanced down the hallway. Light spilled from the room where her voice emanated. Mesmerized by her sweet voice, he suddenly knew that the girl hadn't been lost, just hidden out of view.

A FEW MINUTES LATER, Cyd traipsed into the living room wrapped in a beige towel, her hair wet and tousled. "Your turn," she called out, heading to the plastic bag that contained their fresh clothes.

Good, the shower had rinsed away her mood, Jeffrey thought as he headed down the hallway. Far better for them to be amiable considering he had business to take care of, and Cyd was his means of completing that business.

He doffed his clothes into the appropriate basket before entering the bathroom. The log walls gave the room a cozy feel. Funny how he paid that New York decorator big bucks to renovate his Tribeca loft with a warm, relaxed feel. But all those fabric swatches and custom-mixed colors couldn't compete with the simple, natural warmth created in these cabins.

He stepped into the shower, the glass door squeaking as he closed it behind him. Twisting the knobs, he adjusted the water then grabbed the bar of soap and lathered up, eager to wash off the soot.

Minutes later, he heard a wild racket of noise. He pulled his head out of the spray to hear better. Dogs were barking, people yelling. The room door opened and in slipped Cyd, closing it behind her.

She was dressed in jeans and a chocolate brown pullover that made her dark eyes stand out. Dark eyes that were wide open, glistening with an unspoken message.

She better not have bad news about any missing snowmobile keys. He cracked open the shower door. "What is it?" he asked edgily, anticipating another Cyd surprise.

She smiled and gave a funny little shrug. "I was wondering if you needed anything."

Seeing if he *needed* anything? Momentarily stymied by her response, he stared at her. Couldn't she have waited until he was through showering to ask if he needed anything? But he was learning that boundaries were often blurry, sometimes nonexistent, in the North.

He noticed she was mindlessly running her palms down the sides of her jeans. And her face was flushing.

He didn't have to figure out what really brought her in here. Unless his male compass was off, the lady was aroused. The realization reignited his own hungry desire, which he was damn tired of suppressing. Maybe Cyd could irritate the hell out of him, but she also stirred powerful passions within him like nobody had before.

"You're wondering if I need anything?" he asked, his gaze dropping to her denim pants, their snug fit offering a suggestive view of...every inch of her.

"Yes," she answered hoarsely.

His eyes met hers again. "I think I'm needing exactly what you're needing." He glanced at the door, double-checking it was closed.

Cyd could hardly move. Hardly breathe. She'd come in here with a completely different agenda, but all that melted the moment she saw Jeffrey. He had a way of shaking her up, bad. She, who *never* lost control over a guy, had done it twice within the last hour. The man made her pulse pound, her knees shake, and her palms moist no matter how much she tried to rub them dry against her jeans.

Damn, he looked good naked.

She blew out a nervous gust of breath and checked out the mass of hard tendons and muscle. The swirl of hair that carpeted his pecs, raced down his torso and clung to his muscled diaphragm. And lower, the dark curls couched a very swollen, very impressive member.

I think I'm needing exactly what you're needing.

Her stomach clenched, the tightening working its way down deep between her legs. It had been so long, too long...

When she met his eyes again, they sparkled with hot amusement at her blatant inventory. For a moment she felt silly that she'd stood here and *gawked* at the man. Should she confess she'd been flying solo for months? But when she opened her mouth to speak, nothing came out but a release of breath laced with an achy, needy moan...

"Oh, Cyd, honey," Jeffrey murmured, his throaty voice vibrating throughout her entire being. "Come here." He stepped out of the shower and held out his hand, which glistened with drops of water.

She was hardly aware of walking, just that in the next moment she stood before him, intoxicated by his masculine, soapy scent.

She placed her hand in his.

His skin was warm, wet, and when he closed his hand, hers disappeared. She never felt small in the world, but right now she felt engulfed with Jeffrey's presence and masculinity. And surprise surprise, she *liked* the feeling. It wasn't about being weak, but about feeling safe. Protected. It had never been this way with a man before. Never.

His burning eyes held hers. "You okay?"

"No," she whispered.

"Is this something I shouldn't be doing—"

"No!"

He grinned. "Someday you really should learn to speak your mind."

"Yes." She returned his smile, liking the warmth of their playfulness. An intimacy all their own.

He urged her closer and lowered his mouth to hers. Their warm breaths mingled as his lips grazed hers, brushing featherlight, back and forth. His stubble tickled her cheek.

"Finally I have you," he murmured huskily.

She shuddered as he touched the underside of her top lip with the tip of his tongue. Lightly, sensuously. Then he pulled her into an embrace and pressed his lips full against hers.

Her lips parted on a soft moan as he kissed her.

So this was what it was like to kiss Jeffrey. Hot, slow, exploratory. When his tongue penetrated her mouth, a bolt of pleasure, like lightning, shot through her body. She opened her mouth wider, inviting him inside, tangling her tongue with his as desire electrified every cell of her being.

He flattened the length of her body against his, his body tensing as he molded her to him like a lover.

Her skin burned where his touched hers. Vaguely aware the dampness of his body was soaking through her top, she pulled back and in one movement tugged off her pullover and tossed it aside. Shaking, fighting for breath, she fumbled with the top button on her jeans but stopped when Jeffrey reached out and circled a nipple with his fingertip.

"Your breasts," he murmured thickly, "are so beautiful."

He continued stroking small, sensuous circles around one tightening nub, then the other. She thrust them toward him, gasping from the sheer erotic pleasure of his touch. His eyes were narrowed, solely focused on his fingers tracing slow, measured patterns against her skin. When he plucked a nipple and tugged lightly, she groaned.

"I want to feel you against me," she whispered, pressing forward.

She touched her aching breasts against him, gasping as her sensitized nipples brushed against his chest hair. Flames licked in her belly, threatening to consume her, and she closed her eyes, succumbing to the exquisite heat. Passion had never been like this. Mixed with something more than the body's urgency. If it felt this good already, could she bear the excruciating pleasure of taking him inside her...

Bam bam bam.

Cyd's eyes popped open.

"Someone's at the door," Jeffrey murmured, looking pained.

"Damn," Cyd whispered. "Who's there?" she called out.

"Judy."

"It's the owner," Cyd whispered. "Come on in," she said, raising her voice.

"Hey," Jeffrey said, dropping his hands to cover himself just as a fortyish woman peeked in, her long brown hair falling over her shoulder. "Hi."

"Hi, Judy," Cyd answered. "What's up?"

From fire to ice. Passion to pleasantries. More than mildly stunned, Jeffrey thought once again, how people seemed oblivious to boundaries in this part of the world. Unlike growing up on the streets, where boundaries defined ownership, culture, even language.

"We have a problem," Judy said, looking at Jeffrey.

We? He'd never even met this woman. He nodded, waiting, the rush of water filling the space between Judy's declarations.

"Dogs ate your clothes," she finally said.

It took a moment for the words to penetrate his consciousness. Dogs. Clothes. *"What?"*

"The dogs—"

"Ate my clothes?"

Judy nodded, looking apologetic.

"The clothes in the bag? The clean clothes Geri packed?"

Judy made an affirmative noise. "I don't know if Geri packed them, but yes, they were in a plastic bag."

"Those dogs—" he flashed on them lying near the fire, oblivious to the world "—aren't interested in clothes, just warming themselves at the fireplace!"

"Oh, not *those* dogs," Judy said. "My Husky team. They got into the house. Appears they grabbed the bag of clothes and took it outside." She shook her head regretfully. "I'm sorry."

"I can't let this stop me," he said tightly. "I need to get to the lodge, make a call. I'll just wear my dirty clothes."

If Judy looked apologetic before, she now looked downright woeful. "I already put them in the wash."

"*What?*"

Cyd, who hadn't bothered to cover her breasts, reached behind her and touched Jeffrey's arm in a take-it-easy gesture. "She's efficient, Jeffrey. Can't get mad at her for doing her job."

He choked back an expletive. DNA alteration was nothing compared to the rest of this Alaskan adventure. To hell with modesty. He bunched his hand into a fist and held it against the shower door. "Somebody better come up with a backup plan to this insanity," he growled.

Judy did an unemotional survey of Jeffrey's body. "My husband's about your size," she said. "I think I can find you something to wear." She looked back at Cyd. "And we have some more customers for the shower, so if you don't mind..."

Cyd nodded. "No problem. I'll get out, let him finish up."

Judy smiled. "Thanks."

As the door shut, Cyd smiled sweetly at Jeffrey. "Don't worry. Judy will work things out."

Cyd picked up her top and pulled it over her head.

Snaking her arms into the sleeves, she continued, "I'll go outside and wait for you." After a last adjustment to her top, Cyd headed for the door, pausing before opening it. "Can I get you anything?"

"I'm naked," he said darkly, "hoping somebody named Jerry has something I can wear so I can venture out in godforsaken something-below, to make a call in yet another attempt to conduct business across several thousand miles with a look-alike Alaskan in whose hands rests my entire career. What do you think? Do I need something?"

Cyd waited a beat before speaking. "You get this intense at work, too?" When he didn't answer, she said, "I'll get you a cup of coffee with a shot of whiskey. Trust me, things will look better after that."

"I don't need better, I need *great*," he grumbled. "Make it two shots."

8

THIRTY MINUTES LATER, Cyd—with Jeffrey seated behind her—was steering the snowmobile across the snowy wilderness dotted with evergreens, between the Suds and Showers to the Mush Lodge. She loved this world. Primitive. Vast. Untouched by civilization's dirty hands.

But all that would change if Jeffrey brought his TV series up here. There'd be city types crawling all over, polluting the world with their "conveniences"—more SUVs, TVs, cell phones. They'd probably try to build one of those chain coffee shops, too, and cut in on Charlie's business. Not that Charlie only served coffee, but how could he compete with machines that cranked out lattes and cappuccinos and double-mocha-whipped whatevers?

Jeez, city people sure knew how to complicate a simple cup of java.

Spying a familiar cluster of trees, a landmark the Mush Lodge was near, Cyd eased her grip on the gas. Maybe she could take a quick detour, fake their getting lost.

Bad idea. Jeffrey had ridden this path enough in the last few days to recognize landmarks—he could easily guess she was pulling another fast one. Okay, she wouldn't divert from the path, just drive slower. In the few extra minutes she squeezed out of this ride, she'd figure out some less obvious plan to thwart Jeffrey's goal to radiophone Jordan.

When she shifted a little, Jeffrey's grip tightened around her waist. His arms were big, strong for a city guy. And those hands...

A hot thrill zigzagged through her, followed by sizzling memories of Jeffrey's hands on her breasts...

She sucked in a chilly lungful of air. Dammit anyway. Her goal was to defeat this guy, not desire him.

Think. Think.

The gyrations of the machine weren't helping her think one bit. The vibrations traveled up her legs and settled in a spot between her thighs that suddenly made her bolt upright.

The machine lurched slightly.

Think, dammit.

She'd been able to think clearly earlier when they were cleaning the oilstove. In fact, Cyd had thought through a darn near masterful plan for marooning Jeffrey at the Suds and Showers. Really, it had been pretty brilliant to toss his clean clothes to the sled team, then let inside a few Huskies so Judy and Jerry would have to chase them out.

And in the chaos of the owners corralling dogs, neargenius Cyd had slipped into the shower to play out a little seduction scene to distract Jeffrey, giving the dogs outside ample time to shred and devour his clothes.

But the plan hit a fatal flaw when Cyd got an eyeful

of Jeffrey's naked body. Her sterling genius melted down into brain-numb gimme-some-of-that hots.

Cyd leaned back her head, recalling Jeffrey's searching fingers teasing her, circling fire about her aching nipples...

"Watch out!" Jeffrey yelled.

A tree loomed. Cyd jerked the handle. The machine veered wildly to the left, sliding sideways before she regained control again.

A moment later, after they were motoring back on track, Jeffrey leaned forward and growled against her ear, "Dammit, Cyd! Plenty of room to navigate in this forest, and you head right for a tree?"

"Sorry," she muttered.

"What the hell were you thinking?"

About your burning hands on my hot body. "Nothing."

She wouldn't be playing tree-collision course if Judy hadn't found clothes for Jeffrey to wear. Who'd have thought six-six, three-hundred-pound Jerry had clothes that could fit Jeffrey? Trust Judy to find something. The jeans needed to be rolled up, and the sweater could fit two Jeffreys, but they did the job. He'd been dressed and ready to go minutes after Judy's offer.

The Mush Lodge loomed ahead and Cyd hadn't figured out one devious plan to outwit Jeffrey's call.

A few moments later, Cyd cut the motor and glanced over her shoulder at Jeffrey, taking a moment to look into his hazel eyes through the holes in his ski mask.

Jordan had coached her to soften her rough edges for customer relations. Maybe she should try that with

"Jeffrey relations," too. Up to now, she'd come on like gangbusters in the sexy department, which hadn't really paid off. Not yet. If she wanted to win this game, she'd soften those rough edges, too. Woo the man, weaken him with sizzling sweetness, then pull her next to-be-determined power move. That's probably how city girls behaved to get their man in line.

"I'll get off," Jeffrey said in a strained voice.

Cyd wondered if he thought she'd suddenly restart the motor and careen into the side of the Mush Lodge. After her tree-swerving incident, she couldn't blame the man for being cautious.

She peeked over her shoulder. "If you like," she said, softening any roughness in her voice.

"If I like?"

Recalling a film where Meryl Streep had flirted on a bicycle built for two, Cyd leaned back a little and rubbed her shoulder against Jeffrey's chest. "Whatever you like." Lowering her voice to a growly, I-need-it-bad range, she added, "And whenever you like."

After a pause, Jeffrey croaked, "Why do you always pull this stuff when people are nearby or about to arrive?"

"Next time I'll pull it when we're alone."

Immensely proud of that killer line—Meryl Streep, step aside—Cyd eased off the machine and walked up to the lodge, letting her hips swing way out of their normal range for Jeffrey's benefit.

FIFTEEN MINUTES LATER, Jeffrey strode back to the bar from the radiophone room. He settled on a stool next to Cyd, who was fingering a shot glass of amber liquid.

They hadn't exchanged a word since her little hot come-on outside on the snowmobile. If he was a lesser man, he'd take her up on it in some back room, to hell with people being outside the door. But he'd learned that no matter how fired up she got him, the path of Cyd's motivations wasn't always a straight one. He needed to be cautious, stay centered on why he was here.

So after the hot snowmobile moment, he'd made a beeline inside, and with Charlie's help, had radio-phoned his condo in L.A., guessing Rob and Jordan might still be there, preparing for the meeting. When there'd been no answer, Jeffrey had left several lengthy messages on his service for Jordan, then one on his best pal Rob's as a backup. It was overkill, but Jeffrey had never been a sloppy guy. Better to be thorough and re-petitive than to chance anyone misinterpreting the plan.

After all, today's board meeting would make or break the series. And his career.

Cyd slammed back the shot. After wiping the back of her hand across her lips, she asked, "So Jordan wasn't in?"

"How'd you know?"

"Could hear your conversation out here."

"So you were listening?"

"Everybody listened! It's our local entertainment. Besides, Charlie's turned down the music, so it's easier to hear." She gave a shrug. "Did you know that when you're upset, you enunciate words like some kind of English teacher?"

Jeffrey motioned to Charlie. "Did you know I never planned to be stuck in the middle of bohunk Alaska with my career on the line?"

"Touchy, are we?"

He sliced her a look.

Cyd blinked, looking chastised. "Sorry," she murmured.

Jeffrey frowned. He'd never seen Cyd back down so fast, but didn't have time to ponder it further as Charlie arrived.

"What'll it be, brother?" Charlie's gaze darted over the massive knitted sweater Jeffrey was wearing. "Jerry's?"

He nodded. This world was so small they even knew each other's clothes. "Huskies at the Suds and Showers got into the cabin, ate my clothes."

Charlie quirked a bushy eyebrow. "The sled dogs?"

Jeffrey nodded.

"Sled dogs don't typically get into cabins unless somebody lets them in."

Jeffrey shot a look at Cyd, who was suddenly preoccupied with brushing lint off her parka.

Charlie leaned comfortably against the back of the bar, his red-white-and-blue Peace tattoo flexing over his forearm. "One of your special martinis?"

Jeffrey's attention swung back to the older man. "How'd you get the ingredients with the impending snow front?" If somebody was flying in supplies, he could get a lift out of here.

"Didn't," Charlie said, setting a shot glass in front of Jeffrey and filling it with whiskey. "That's why it's special. For you, only." He chuckled to himself. "I'll offer one to Jordan when he's back. That'll shake up the beer-lovin' guy."

"Shake him up, but don't stir." Jeffrey smiled wryly and lifted his drink. "To your health, Charlie."

"Likewise, brother." Charlie glanced at Cyd, who was still busy fixing something on her parka, then winked at Jeffrey.

He knows I have a handful on my hands with this little dynamo.

Jeffrey had always prided himself on his smooth handling of the opposite sex, but his techniques were sorely challenged by Cyd. Most women he'd known played it subtle, feigning little moods he could easily anticipate and act accordingly to remain in control.

Not with Cyd. Jeffrey was constantly on the alert, trying to figure out what the hell was coming next. Or what had gone on before—like what was the *real* story with Judy and Jerry's dogs getting into the cabin?

Or what was with that little teasing number Cyd had pulled on the snowmobile before coming in here? He'd seen her naked body pressed brazenly against glass, watched her boldly enter his shower room. But that come-get-me-bad-boy act on the snowmobile was a new one. What was she up to?

"So who's Ashley?"

Jeffrey turned his head and caught Cyd's glistening eyes filled with questions.

"You heard that, too?"

"Not all of it. Harry was boasting about a caribou he bagged so I only caught the part about Jordan needing to steer clear of her."

"Didn't you have anything better to do than listen to my private conversation?"

"Private? *Everybody* heard. So who's Ashley?"

Everybody? Jeffrey downed the whiskey, liking the kick-ass rush of warmth. He might as well answer. God knows Cyd wouldn't stop asking. "The wrong lady for Jordan to tangle with," he answered, putting down the glass. "Not if he wants to live and tell about it."

"You underestimate Jordan," she snapped. She paused, then continued in a warmer, friendlier voice. "He once chased off a grizzly from some unsuspecting tourists. Trust me, he can tangle with a city girl and live to tell about it."

"What our pal Jordan doesn't know is that Ashley *is* part grizzly." He signaled Charlie for another drink. "Wish I'd had a chance to ask Jordan if he had any last minute questions about the annual report, the organization..." Damn and double damn. Jeffrey had never been thousands of miles from a critical meeting, with his career in the hands of a stranger. His saving grace was his best pal Rob, who'd done plenty of film work for Argonaut and knew its business and employees. He'd left Jordan Rob's phone numbers, and vice versa, so the two of them could connect. Rob would do whatever it took to help Jordan be successful.

Plus, Jeffrey had to remember that nobody at Argonaut had seen him in a year. It wouldn't be so strange if he, well Jordan, looked a little rougher, maybe forgot a face or stumbled over a name.

Easing in a long, slow breath, Jeffrey mindlessly scratched his chin, feeling the bristle of his growing beard. *And I'm hoping Jordan looks like me? Hell, I'm starting to look like him.*

This bizarre switcheroo is just a twenty-four hour thing, Jeffrey reminded himself. *Twenty-four hours and it'll all be over.*

"Sorry you're having such a rough day."

Dropping his hand, he looked into Cyd's eyes. "I'm not accustomed to getting so filthy dirty I have to commute to a shower where a pack of dogs eat my clothes." He narrowed his eyes, scrutinizing her reaction.

She smiled sweetly. "I guess in New York or L.A. you wash up at home with a poodle lounging in its own doggie room."

What a little actress, now playing the innocent. "Minus the poodle and doggie room, you got it right."

"No poodle? What, then? Beagle? Scottie?"

"Neither. I'm not home enough to take care of a pet."

"Then why have a home?"

As Charlie refilled his glass, Jeffrey shot Cyd a questioning look. "What?"

"Why have a home if it's just for one person. Why not rent a room in someone else's home?"

He lifted his drink. "Uh, I like my privacy?"

"You mean, you like being alone."

"I'm alone out of necessity, not choice." He paused,

startled at that bit of self-realization. *Choice?* He hadn't chosen this life. It had been foisted on him as long as he could remember. One foster family after another, none of them places where he belonged even if the state had the balls to call them foster "homes."

You like being alone.

He'd never really given it a whole lot of thought, just vaguely accepted he'd always be the kind of man who lived his life alone. Accepted he'd never belong to a family. He'd never thought there was a choice...but now that he did, his gut ached with an emptiness he didn't want to acknowledge.

He tossed back the whiskey, then set the glass down roughly on the bar. "Let's go," he said gruffly.

LATER THAT AFTERNOON, Cyd eased the snowmobile to a stop in front of the Mush Lodge. Jeffrey had been near-rabid to hear the results of his board meeting, so here she was making yet another trip back.

A team of sled dogs barked and howled at the new arrival and for a moment Cyd envied their freedom of expression. Ever since her and Jeffrey's earlier visit to the lodge, Cyd had been on her best behavior. No, better than merely best. She'd been so sweet and easy-going, Geri had worried Cyd was coming down with the flu.

Cyd had assured her aunt she felt fine, not admitting she was acting city-girl like—or what she presumed to be city-girl like—to woo Jeffrey into trusting her more.

Cyd cut the engine. "We're here," she said sweetly.

Jeffrey slid off and stood next to the snowmobile. "You okay? You've been acting...different."

She smiled under her ski mask. "Fine. Fine." She gestured toward the gray clouds on the horizon. "Make it quick. Another storm front's coming."

"Geri said she heard on the radio it'd be several hours before it hit."

Cyd contemplated applying a hammer to her aunt's clock radio when they got back. "Yeah, well, the news isn't foolproof." She looked at the skies, pretending to analyze it. "In my expert opinion, I say we should leave now."

"Now? We just got here!" Jeffrey looked at some parked snowmobiles. "Why aren't they leaving?"

"They're probably staying overnight at the lodge," she lied.

"It's imperative I make that call. I'll make it fast, then we'll get back to Geri's." All business, he turned and strode toward the lodge.

A few moments later, she shoved open the heavy wooden door just as Charlie was calling across the room to Jeffrey, "Glad to see you, brother. Jordan radioed. Said the meeting's postponed until Friday and to call him at his—I mean *your*—office. Told Jordan weather's howling, but that's before it broke. News report says the next wave won't hit for another two hours, so you have plenty of time to call him back."

Jeffrey looked at Cyd, who became absorbed in removing her parka.

"Oh, and he asked what you did to Ashley," Charlie added.

Jeffrey muttered an expletive and made a beeline to the radio room.

Cyd stood, feeling an icky feeling in the pit of her stomach. *Ashley.* Jeffrey had said she wasn't the type of lady to tangle with. Cyd still didn't know what that meant, but now that Jordan was asking what Jeffrey "had done" to Ashley, well, it seemed pretty obvious Jeffrey and this Ashley person were an item.

With an indignant roll of her shoulders, she stomped to the bar. Straddling a seat, she grumbled to Charlie, "Get me a whiskey."

"What's wrong, Juliet?" asked Harry, nursing a beer.

"Shut up." She felt a ripple of guilt. After all, Harry had loaned her his snowmobile. "Uh, thanks for letting me use your machine."

Harry muttered something about always being there to help out, but his words faded as other thoughts crowded her mind.

Jeffrey could've told me about Ashley.

Not that he owed her explanations of his dating habits, but jeez, Cyd had been *naked* in front of the man two and a half times! He could've had the decency to mention the other woman after the first time!

Charlie set a filled shot glass in front of Cyd. "You okay, hon?"

"Peachy." She downed the drink and nodded to Charlie she wanted another.

He hesitated, then refilled it. When Cyd raised it to her lips, she heard pieces of Jeffrey's conversation over the radiophone with someone named "Bonnie." How many women did this man juggle at once?

She tossed back the second whiskey and banged the glass on the bar.

Charlie, making a pot of coffee, barely looked in her direction. "Sorry, Cyd. I'm cutting you off."

"What? I've only had two!"

"I've known you for almost ten years, and I know when you're hell-bent to cause trouble. I'm saving you from yourself."

"And the rest of the bar," Harry said with a chuckle.

Cyd glowered at the men who were laughing. "I replaced the mirror and chairs."

"And we don't want to replace them again," Charlie said gently, setting a steaming mug of coffee in front of her.

"You'd think after five years, the jokes would stop," she muttered. But even she knew with scarce local entertainment, that wild antic like hers would live on forever. She'd only been twenty and it had been a bad day. A DeHavilland she'd been flying had been grounded, and she hadn't found the mechanical failure. Later, she'd accidentally found Harry with what's-her-face. No mechanical failure, there. Frustrated at the plane and pissed off at Harry, Cyd had visited the Mush Lodge, had a few too many and taken out her rage on some inanimate objects which took a month's wages to replace.

She'd never lost it like that since. Probably because she learned that just as one could always fly another plane, a girl could always find another guy. Six months later she'd been kicking it up with a fellow bush pilot, Tim Carolan. And six months after that...hell, that guy's name escaped her now.

Ever since then, that had been her romance track record. Rollicking lust that slid into friendship. Intimacy was more about having fun than anything else. Not all that challenging or soul-shaking.

Until she met Jeffrey.

Cyd wrapped her hands around the warm mug. Of all the men to get to her, how'd it end up being a city slicker? She was accustomed to tough men up here in the North, but Jeffrey was more than that. A combination of brain smarts and body brawn. Throw in that civilized edge of his, and she was definitely off balance.

Plus, he reminded her of the world she'd left behind so long ago. One filled with stories and dreams. The way he'd asked questions while they were cleaning the stove had at first irked her, but deep down, that kind of camaraderie reminded her of those long talks she'd have with her dad late at night while they were closing up the movie theater. Long, meandering discussions on everything from their favorite cartoon strips to how her father had invoked Egyptian history in his beloved theater.

Jeffrey's probably like that.

And in a moment of intense yearning, Cyd imagined falling into a pocket of time where she and Jeffrey wouldn't have their guards up. They'd talk and laugh easily. She bet he knew a lot about things like literature and art. And she'd surprise him with her knowledge of film and how once upon a time she'd dreamed of being a movie star and he'd laugh, but he'd be smart enough to know she really meant she'd once believed in a life where there was no pain or want...

Emotion stung her eyes and she raised the cup to her lips and sipped, not wanting the guys to see her vulnerability.

Minutes later, Jeffrey strode back into the bar area. The men turned quiet as he headed past them to a stool next to Cyd. Sitting down, Jeffrey smiled tightly at Charlie. "Special martini, please."

Charlie complied, setting a shot glass in front of Jeffrey.

The bar was so quiet, Cyd could hear one of the dogs snoring. "Who's Bonnie?" she finally asked.

"Bonnie?" answered Jeffrey, shifting her a look. "That's my secretary. I could tell Jordan hadn't clued her in as to his real identity, so I pretended I was myself and asked some questions." He blew out a gust of air. "This is getting too complicated. I *am* myself. What am I pretending?"

"Who's Rob?" asked one of the guys.

Jeffrey did a double take down the bar. "Uh, my best friend back in L.A." He turned to Cyd and whispered, "Did *everyone* listen in?"

"Like I told you, local entertainment." Cyd ran her fingers along worn wooden bar top, feeling the carved names of loves and dates gone by.

Another man's voice piped up. "Hey, Jeff. You need to trust Jordan more and stop worrying about his pulling off this presentation thing."

This was followed by general sounds of agreement.

Jeffrey, holding his drink midair, turned his attention to the men sitting at the end of the bar. "That was a private call."

"Think again," someone said.

A rippling of baritone laughter.

Jeffrey rubbed his fingers around the edge of the glass. In New York or L.A. he never had to deal with bar types commenting on his business transactions. "Overhearing a conversation doesn't mean it's everyone's business," he said solemnly.

"Nothing's private if it affects all of us," Cyd countered.

He shot her a look. "What?"

"You heard me."

The only sound was the crackling of the fire and the ragged snoring of a dog. Something caught Jeffrey's eye on the bar where Cyd's hand lay. Scratched into the wood were the darkened words "Harry loves Cyd."

Harry?

The guy who ran the sled team that brought them here from the airstrip?

"What affects you," Jeffrey said, feeling edgy and knowing it was over more than this discussion, "is also good for you." He downed his drink, not liking the dark tangle of emotions within him.

"Bull." Cyd jumped off her stool and strolled down the line of men until she stood right in the middle of them. "You know what he's bringing to our world, don't you?"

There were a few grunts. Someone asked "What?"

"Big business," Cyd answered, fisting her hands on her hips. "It's our enemy."

Ominous grumblings.

"You know what big business brings, don't you?" This time she didn't wait for any answers. "Pollution. Lost jobs. Disease."

"Disease?" Jeffrey stood, disbelieving this little speech Cyd was working up. An iron band seemed to tighten around his forehead as he headed toward her.

Ignoring Jeffrey, she continued, "Yes, disease. The kind big cities breed. Was this film series invited here? No. Did we say we wanted, no *needed*, them to help our economy, our lifestyle? No!"

Jeffrey was a bit stunned that she'd spat the words "film series" as though they were pure evil, but he didn't have time to ponder this. The locals were getting restless. Men were glaring at him, muttering things he was glad he couldn't clearly hear. And Cyd, well, there was a one-eighty personality switch. The recent sweet, amenable woman had turned into a wild, rabble-rousing riot maker.

Another storm front had hit, and it had nothing to do with the weather outside.

"Gentlemen," Jeffrey said.

"Who the hell's he talkin' to?" someone barked.

Loud guffaws and bar thumping.

Jeffrey strode to a spot near Cyd, positioning himself as though this were a debate. "Good men of the North," he said, correcting the salutation, "Cyd's right."

He knew *that* proclamation would leave her open-mouthed. Which was what he wanted. To stun her into silence for a few moments.

"Yes, she's absolutely right," he continued. "In the past, big business has been thoughtless and cavalier, bringing with it pollution, lost jobs, disease. But that's not what I'm bringing." He lowered his voice to a brotherly tone. "I bring opportunities. Not only to Arctic Luck, where the series would be based, but to other communities such as Katimuk, too, because we'll be filming in different areas, needing different resources."

Somebody snorted.

"These opportunities I speak of will bring useful services to your community—" Jeffrey recalled the ribbon of dirt that sufficed for a runway "—such as paving that landing strip outside town."

The room grew quiet.

"And I think Judy and Jerry would appreciate the funding to build a second shower—I've heard the wait gets up to two hours." He didn't dare look at Cyd as she'd given him that piece of information.

"And then there's no hot water," someone chimed in.

"And as to lost jobs, the TV series would do just the opposite. It would bring jobs."

"Such as?" one of the men snarled.

"Such as positions for cooks, carpentry, more sled teams, even extras," answered Jeffrey.

"Extra what?" one of them men asked.

"I'll have an extra shot!" Someone banged a glass on the bar.

More laughter.

Jeffrey overrode the turbulence. "Locals would get paid to dress up and walk across a sound stage for money. Imagine, getting paid to just walk across a room. That's like free money."

In the weighty silence, Jeffrey knew he had the advantage. He figured he'd just successfully wooed at least eighty percent of his audience.

"And best of all," he said, moving closer to the men, being one of them. "It's temporary. For a short time—a year, possibly more if the series is successful, of course—but in the long run, it's a business that eventually leaves your state. But also leaves behind communities that gained income, services, even benefits such as the studios' health clinics."

This last part was inspired by Cyd's claim big business brought "disease." But he could certainly make it part of the negotiated package that additional funding would be channeled into the medical clinics, which would offer services to the local people as well.

"We could use those things," someone muttered.

"Yeah, we gotta hike to Anchorage if we need a hospital."

"Hear, hear."

No laughter. No sardonic asides. Maybe a few questioning looks, but the rest of the men were open-faced, smiling. Jeffrey warmed with the realization he'd not only won the argument, he'd won their hearts.

He looked at Cyd's furious scowl.

That is, all except one heart.

9

STEERING THE SNOWMOBILE across the snow, Cyd entertained dark thoughts of hitting a bump at full speed, causing Jeffrey to lose his grip and fly off into a snowbank. Maybe such a jolt would knock some sense into him.

But she doubted it. Not into Mr. City Slicker, I-Bring-Opportunities-to-Alaska Jeffrey Bradshaw. He was too opinionated, too *hardheaded*, for such an impact to have any effect.

Damn him anyway. One-upping her in front of all the guys back at the lodge, giving that rousing speech about all the "opportunities" he'd be bringing to Alaska with that TV series. Who did Jeffrey think he was? Jimmy Stewart in *Mr. Smith Goes to Washington*? After the big movie chain had moved into her old neighborhood of Seattle, and her dad had tried to salvage his theater by turning it into an art film house, he'd played that classic film. There hadn't been much of an audience, except Cyd, who saw it at least eight times.

She hadn't been prepared to see it again today at the lodge, with Jeffrey playing the noble advocate of what's best for the people.

She thumbed the throttle. The engine revved higher,

matching her rising fury at the locals for buying into Jeffrey's bull. Mush Lodge was aptly named. Because that's what her pals' brains had turned into. *Mush.* Sure, life could be tough in the North, but if they didn't like it, they could pack their Gore-Tex and hightail to the lower forty-eight and let the *real* Alaskans appreciate and protect the last frontier.

Cyd looked at the overcast sky. Gray clouds, the next onslaught of the storm, hovered on the horizon. That's how Jeffrey's series was...hovering darkly in the distance, ready to descend and wreak havoc. It was so obvious—didn't people see?

Fools.

An inukshuk, the piled stones looking like a squat woman, appeared to the right.

The landmark to an old favorite haunt where a teenaged Cyd had often escaped while visiting her aunt. Fresh from Seattle, Cyd had called the refuge the "White Palace"—a name she'd stolen from a movie although her sanctuary had nothing to do with the film. Cyd had simply liked the words because that's how her secret place looked in winter—white, majestic. She'd felt safe and protected there. Able to let down her guard and feel the things she hid from others. Especially the things about her father.

Suddenly, with a yearning that bordered on desperation, Cyd jerked the handles and steered back to the inukshuk.

"What are you doing?" Jeffrey yelled, pressing against her back.

She ignored him. He'd had his chance to talk back at

the lodge, she didn't owe him a listening audience anymore.

As they sped down a ravine she caught snippets of Jeffrey's words in the air.

"Where—?"

"Why—?"

"The storm—"

She didn't answer, kept driving. The next storm front wasn't going to hit for an hour or so. They could spare a few minutes to see the White Palace.

If Jeffrey's city-ness hadn't made him immune to life's simple pleasures, maybe the beauty of the place would touch him, too. Yes, suddenly her spontaneous mission had a double reason. Solace for her, inspiration for him. Well, maybe. But it was worth the shot. Maybe he'd get a sense of what this land was about, maybe he'd want to protect it, maybe, maybe, maybe.

A few minutes later, she rounded a small hill and entered a secluded meadow glazed with snow.

The White Palace.

The trees were dusted with frost, the iced leaves and branches like floating lace as the wind pushed through the trees. Far off, a wolf howled. She eased the machine to a stop, keeping the motor on for the heat it blew back. That, and the heated seat and handles, made the stop reasonably comfortable.

"What are you doing?" Jeffrey repeated edgily.

She didn't turn around, just kept staring at the world of lace and magic, white so pure it hurt her eyes. "It's beautiful, isn't it?"

"Is that why we're here? Because it's beautiful?"

She should have known he was immune. "Isn't that enough?"

She swung her leg over the machine and jumped to the ground, feeling antsy and furious. The powder kicked up as she trudged away from Mr. City Slicker, hating him for being so ignorant of what really mattered.

"Cyd!"

"Go blow," she muttered to herself.

"Cyd, dammit! Get back here!"

She stopped, her breaths burning in her throat. Who the hell did he think he was? Just because he gave that eat-out-of-my-hand speech at the lodge, did he think *she* was at his beck and call, too?

With a renewed burst of energy, she spun around and stomped back. It was time to blast this guy, level his pompous, self-serving self.

She reached the snowmobile, stopped and whipped off her ski mask, wanting Jeffrey to fully witness her rage.

Behind the holes in his mask, she saw his eyes widen. Good. *Take a long look, buddy. You're seeing the other people in this world, the ones you didn't wow in the lodge. The ones who don't buy your line.*

The ones who don't want you here.

"What is this about?" he finally asked.

"Something you never do."

"Hello?"

"You never appreciate this country's splendor."

"What?" He looked around, then returned his gaze

to hers. "Same view through Geri's window. Let's enjoy it from there."

"It all looks the same to you? This is—" she opened her arms wide "—one of the most beautiful places I know. A secret, magical place I'd go to as a girl, and you think it's like *any* view from *any* window?" She dropped her hands against her sides. "Where do you find beauty in the city? In a bank? In a fancy latte-mocha shop with some skinny, uptight..." She chewed on her bottom lip, stopping herself from asking—while they were accidentally on the topic—just who the hell Ashley and Bonnie were.

Nearby, a gray jay perched on a high branch chattered incessantly, seemingly as irritated as Cyd.

Jeffrey tugged off his ski mask and huffed an exasperated breath, releasing a plume of vapor into the air. "Sometimes you are so..." He gave his head a shake. "Get back on the machine. Let's go home."

She fisted her hands on her hips. "Don't order me around."

"Cyd, I'm not trying to order—"

"Like hell!" She choked back a laugh. "You want to order all of us around!"

"That's ridiculous. I'd be a fool to order anyone around, *especially* you."

"Oh, not just the obvious 'do this, do that' kind of orders," she continued, speaking over his words, "but 'here's money, build a new airstrip' kind of devious orders—"

"Those aren't orders—"

"You think people will be so happy getting free

money—isn't that what you called it? *Free* money?—that they won't question the damage you'll bring to our world?" Suddenly her chest ached. She felt as though her past and her future were colliding, smashing everything she'd cherished.

"Cyd, it's cold out here—"

"It's twenty below!"

"That's cold!"

"That's a *little* chilly!" She was losing it. She sounded shrill and felt irrational as hell. Wanting to regain control of herself, and the situation, she stopped talking and flashed Jeffrey a dare-you look.

Which he met with a steely one. In a hard-forced calm, he said, "This is really about your blaming me for Jordan not being here—"

"Oh, screw that. I concocted that story to cover up the *real* reason you piss me off!"

"Same as concocting the 'dogs accidentally ran into the cabin' story?"

"I didn't have to concoct that. I just opened the damn door!"

Jeffrey had often compared Cyd to a weather system, and finally, her storm front had hit in all its fury. But it didn't deter him. He welcomed it because now was his opportunity to finally learn what the hell was behind her push-and-pull, hot-and-cold tactics.

"All right," he said evenly, folding his arms over his chest. "Spill. What have I done to...piss you off?"

"Your TV series."

"Why?"

"Because...it'll destroy our world."

"So *that's* why you think I'm your enemy?"

"I said...big business is."

"But that's what you *think,* isn't it? That *I'm* your enemy."

He caught a flash of acknowledgment in her eyes.

"What about the pleasure the stories of this land would bring people? Surely you of all people can relate to that. Isn't that what you did as a girl? Escape into such stories in your father's theater?"

"That's none of your business." She looked as though she was going to add something, then suddenly dipped her head and stared at the ground.

Jeffrey waited for her to bounce back, bark something else about his motives or his "enemy" status.

Nothing.

He tried to see the look on her face. Probably still giving him that go-to-hell look, but difficult to see with her head bowed like that. But her voice had changed. It had sounded softer, oddly disconcerting. Not like the brash Cyd he'd grown accustomed to.

That's when he saw the shimmer of tears beneath the thick dark crescent of her lashes.

"Sorry," he said quietly, struggling for words. He, who could wield language like a weapon in negotiations, couldn't come up with more than a single word to express what lay in his heart.

That the last thing he'd ever do was hurt her.

He'd been quiet so long, Cyd finally looked up, anguish pinching her delicate features. She made an elaborate display of brushing her mittened hand against her hair, swiping the corner of her eye in the process.

"Let's go home," he urged. "We can talk more there."

"No," she whispered.

Jeffrey thought back to Geri's words. *Cyd seemed afraid to stop being the family caretaker. As though if she let go, everything would fall apart.*

Was that what this was about? Her letting go? Maybe what scared Cyd the most was what Jeffrey symbolized, not what he might bring to her world. Because deep down, what she really didn't want touched was the memory of what had been.

The memory, he'd wager, she clung to and protected with the ferocity of a mama bear. Refused to let go of.

The memory of her family—intact—while her father had been alive.

No way he could broach that topic. Not now. His eyes searched hers, recalling something else Geri had said. *I swore that little girl would grow up to be a movie star the way she lived and breathed films.*

He didn't want to hurt her, but this subject had already been touched on. It was the only way he could make her understand he had good intentions.

"You think the series will destroy your world, and yet...you grew up loving movies."

She looked at him oddly and affirmed with the faintest nod of her head. In the distance, another howl.

"Think about it. The world I create is that world you love. Or once loved. Seems to me that connects, not divides us. That hardly makes me your enemy."

For a moment, Cyd's face held such vulnerability, he

didn't dare say another word for fear one more thing could break her.

Then events changed so swiftly he barely comprehended what happened. She moved forward, almost imperceptibly. He opened his arms. The next he knew, she fell into him, clutching him tightly, her chest heaving with silent sobs.

Stunned, he simply held her. He'd comforted crying women before, but this was different. Cyd wasn't the kind of woman to cave into her emotions—well, the more vulnerable kind. For her to let down her guard meant she'd dropped her act.

She trusted him.

He brushed a kiss across her forehead, her hair, infused with the sudden urge to coddle her, protect her—*Cyd* of all women!—but the feelings burning within him were sweeter, more compelling than anything he'd ever experienced with a woman. "Cyd, sweetheart," he murmured over and over, his hands molding her to him, gathering her deeper into his embrace.

Nestled in the crook of his neck, Cyd sucked up her emotions, literally. Dammit. Tears were freezing to her face. She never cried, not like this. But this man had a way of pushing her to the edge, infuriating the hell out of her. And the next moment, saying something that sliced right down to her soul. Yes, she'd loved movies. They'd been the key to her childhood dreams. Geri divulged that tidbit no doubt. Minutes ago, Cyd would have felt her aunt's divulgence a betrayal. Consorting with the enemy.

But in the shelter of Jeffrey's embrace, Cyd felt... well, differently.

For one thing, she was overwhelmed with the sensation of his body against hers. How his hands rubbed her back in comforting caresses, the way he kissed her brow, murmuring sweet words. She felt warm and safe and...

Aroused.

She lifted her face, taking in his scent—wondering idly when it had become so achingly familiar—and inched her mouth over his jaw. The prickle of his beard was rough, electrifying, against her lips...

And her enemy became her lover as she sought his lips and pressed her mouth against his as though he could breath life into those dreams again.

Jeffrey, still straddling the machine, tugged her closer, consuming Cyd's lips. So tender. And oh so soft. When her tongue eased between his lips, he groaned at the taste of her. Heat. Whiskey.

His mouth moved to the corner of her lips. "We should go," he murmured.

"You kidding?"

In a rush of movement, she clamped her hands on either side of his head, pinning him in place as she pressed her lips to his, making love with her tongue and lips in wild abandon as though she had every right to claim what's hers.

In the midst of kissing and grappling and moaning, some corner of his mind fought to keep things in check. A daunting challenge considering his hot, pulsing erection was telegraphing urgent needs that threatened to raze any lingering thoughts of sanity.

And sanity was paramount considering naked bodies and frigid air didn't mix well. With superhuman effort, he pulled his head away and gasped, "Go. We should go."

"Where?"

"Caribbean."

"What?"

"*Cabin*. Meant to say cabin."

"Why?"

"Too...cold...here." His breath exploded from his lungs as she kneaded him through his pants. "Oh...Cyd..." It felt so good. Damn good. "We'll get frostbite."

Suckling his earlobe, she whispered feverishly, "Not if we're quick."

That did it.

Quick? So much adrenaline was rushing through him, at the moment he could run a one-minute mile.

Beneath him the snowmobile was warm and vibrating...

"Get on the machine," he growled.

He wasn't sure if he tossed her there or if she jumped, but suddenly there she was, facing him, straddling the machine and sucking face with the intensity of a one-woman marauding army. Grappling with the outside of her parka, he found two mounds and rubbed and stroked and squeezed.

The machine started bucking.

He yanked his head away, praying to God a passing

bull moose didn't think this snowmobile looked a little sexy, when he saw the source of the movement.

Cyd leaned forward, streams of vapor escaping her swollen, panting lips as she ground her pelvis against the leather seat. Her eyes locked with his, she widened her thighs and increased the pace of her rubbing.

"Cyd, Lord, I want to..."

She sat up and grabbed the zipper on her jacket. *Rrr-iii-p.*

She tore it off and tossed it aside, but he caught it midair.

"Are you crazy?" he yelled.

Obviously yes, because now she *stood* on the seat, unzipped her pants and tugged them down. Right at eye level, he choked back a groan at the sight of her pink-gold skin and patch of dark sex.

When he looked up and caught that steamy, what're-you-gonna-do-about-it look, he knew *exactly* what he'd do.

Quickly he wrapped the parka around her bare bottom. "Come here, baby," he growled, pulling her cleft to him. "Cover me up."

Darkness enveloped his head inside the parka.

Her scent permeated the dark warmth. Tangy, sweet. He slipped his tongue into her crevice, a needy moan reverberating in his throat as he tasted her. Grabbing her buttocks, he held her in place as he licked the inside of her slick folds, up and down.

Then he inched his tongue up to the nub and flicked it.

Her thighs quivered.

Holding her in place with one hand, he grazed his other up her thigh and slid his fingers inside her crevice.

Pumping her slightly, he suckled her nub greedily.

Her hips rotated slightly in tight, spasmodic motions as he pumped and licked and sucked. When she spread her knees wider, he penetrated her more deeply, his tongue laving the pearl in the tangle of wet curls. After a moment, the hungry movements of her hips stilled and she stiffened, then cried out his name.

When he felt her body relax, he pulled his head out of the parka. Looking up he saw Cyd panting, a glazed look in her eyes.

Leaning back on the seat, he unzipped his fly. "Sit on me."

She looked down, her eyes darkening with arousal. In one swift motion, she kicked out of one pant leg and lowered herself. He guided his shaft to her opening. Crouching, she sank slowly down.

As her tight, silky heat enveloped him, he squeezed shut his eyes and emitted a deep, prolonged groan. Normally he'd take it slow, but her muscled legs were exposed outside the parka still tossed over her. He grasped her hips underneath the coat and buried himself in her in one controlled motion.

"Oh...Lord...Cyd." Sweet, hot need coiled tight within him. He drove himself deeper. She cried out as he filled her completely.

"Baby, ride me."

For a narrow seat, Cyd was creative. She'd braced the sole of one foot on the seat, and crossed her other leg behind her. Amazingly she sat astride him with ease, raising her hips up and down, sliding along his rigid sex. Through an opening in her parka, he caught flashes of her sweet cleft, pink and wet and exposed, slapping against him.

"That's it, baby. Harder, faster." Engorged to the point of pain, he drove deeper against her movements.

Her head suddenly fell back and she wailed her release. As her insides convulsed spasmodically, he thrust hard. Once. Twice. Then his hips shot off the seat as he exploded into her, flooded with wave after wave of excruciating pleasure. Finally, with a shudder of satisfaction, he collapsed back on the seat and Cyd fell on top of him, their warm breaths mingling.

Afterward, they dressed in silence. When Jeffrey started to sit on the back part of the seat, Cyd motioned him to the front.

"You drive," she said.

"You ordering me around?"

"Hell yes," she whispered.

And she did, all the way back to Geri's. Telling Jeffrey to feather the throttle, take it easy on the brake lever. And he didn't tell her he'd driven one of these before because he liked the feel of her arms wound comfortably around his waist and how her head rested against his back.

He liked her trusting him.

And he didn't tell her that as they left her secret place, he saw its beauty in the snow-crusted leaves and the chattering jay.

But most of all, he saw it in her.

10

JEFFREY STIRRED AWAKE to the scent of coffee. Blinking open his eyes, he saw Babette stretched in front of the woodstove, the flames crackling softly. Outside the far window, he watched the snow fall in fat flakes against the glass.

It was cold out there.

Or, as Cyd might say, "a little chilly."

Remembering her line from yesterday, he closed his eyes and smiled, inching a bit closer to the soft curve of her back. He liked how their bodies spooned. A natural, comfortable fit as though they'd been doing this for years.

In a sense, this was their first private moment since returning to the cabin yesterday. After that, he, Geri and Cyd had spent the evening preparing dinner, washing dishes, investigating the source of a mysterious draft, then over a late-night hot cocoa, discussing Geri's options for buying a new generator.

At bedtime, Geri had trundled off to her room and Cyd and Jeffrey had taken to the sofa. His last memories were lying in the dark, listening to the crackling fire, and realizing from the weight of Cyd's head on his shoulder that she'd fallen asleep. When a distant clock had chimed midnight, he drowsily recalled it was his birthday. In the past, a day that typically felt like nothing more than a new day.

But this time, it felt like a new beginning.

Cyd rustled, yawned. She reached behind her, her touch feathery against his thigh. He interlaced his fingers with hers and leaned close to her ear.

"Good morning, sleepyhead."

She giggled lazily. "Morning."

She pulled his hand around to her front and held it cushioned against her breasts. They lay quietly, staring out the window at the falling snow, and he had a sudden, giddy sense of their looking into the future together.

Some part of him balked. Being tied to someone wasn't his style. Even when he'd been engaged five years ago, he'd known it was a mistake. She'd been willing to move, give up her career, but in his heart he didn't want her to change her life for him. She was a good woman, but a chameleon to his needs and it had felt empty to him.

But being with Cyd was different. Life with her was exhilarating, passionate. She was a daredevil, a woman to be reckoned with. And although the two of them had grown up in totally different environments, at a rock-deep level they were the same. He'd thought before how they shared a knowledge about survival one only learns on the streets or in the wilderness. They were two parts of a whole, together creating something that was bigger than themselves, bigger than the world.

And he wondered if that something was love.

She shifted and turned, her body like warm liquid against his. Her skin was like silk over muscle. Her fragrance sweet, familiar.

She pressed her face against his chest and kissed him softly over his heart. The touch of her lips sent a rush of heat through him. He brushed his lips against her hair, catching the scent of pine and smoke, then inched his mouth to her ear.

"I want to take you," he whispered hotly.

Where his hand lay on her bottom, he felt a misting of goose bumps on her skin as she squirmed a little.

"Take me where?" she murmured.

"To paradise."

"But we're weathered in."

He gave her buttock a soft pinch and she giggled sleepily.

A form shadowed the window. He looked up.

Geri stood in front of the window, draped in a loose shirt over pants. After glancing at the back of Cyd's head nestled against Jeffrey's chest, Geri looked at him and smiled.

For a moment, he felt awkward. Not red-faced embarrassed like when she'd caught him on the enclosed deck with Cyd, buttons and guilt everywhere. This moment was just...awkward. He really was a more sophisticated guy than to be caught in compromising situations in his host's home.

But Geri seemed oblivious to any discomfort. She flashed a toothy grin. "Ready for breakfast?"

AN HOUR LATER THEY SAT at the breakfast table. Geri, in the middle of slathering jam on a slice of bread, suddenly looked out the window and said, "Buddy would've gotten a kick out of this."

Cyd, her fork piled high with a stack of bacon, toast and egg, held it midair. "Out of what?"

"That fox over there..." Geri pointed her knife out the window at a red fox crouched low in the snow, stealthily approaching Geri's snowmobile. "Probably smells some lingering scents of the moose meat I carted over to Calvin's yesterday. Buddy had a soft spot for animals, 'member? No doubt I would've had to give my little brother a lecture or two about not feeding the wildlife."

Now that the storm had subsided again, they could see out the window. The world was frosted white, the sky overcast. Gusts of wind blew puffs of snow off the trees.

"Yeah, Dad would've had to learn that pets are dogs and horses, not foxes and bears. He was a gentle soul. A real Libra." Cyd stuffed the forkful of food into her mouth, savoring the mix of flavors and grease.

"What're you?" asked Geri, glancing at Jeffrey.

"A fox?" he quipped.

Cyd chewed, smiling to herself. After their snowmobile tryst yesterday, she'd tag him as a wolf. Wild, fierce, ravenous. They were loyal, too, wolves. Mated for life. She felt a fluttering in her chest that took her by surprise. Not that it mattered what Jeffrey was doing for the rest of his life.

"No," Geri said, "I mean, what sign are you?"

Jeffrey blew on his coffee. "Libra."

"What a coincidence!" said Geri. "What day?"

Jeffrey paused. "Sixteenth."

Geri did a double take. "That's today!"

He shrugged. "I've never been one to celebrate my birthday."

Cyd observed how his eyes clouded over, as though distancing himself from the topic.

"Well, Good God, Jeff!" Geri exclaimed. "Why didn't ya say something? I'd have made a special breakfast!"

Jeffrey looked around the table. "Bacon, eggs, home-made bread, coffee, oatmeal, raisins, brown sugar." He looked back at Geri. "If this isn't special, I don't know what is."

With a grunt, Geri pushed back her chair, scraping it against the hardwood floor. She stood and headed to the kitchen.

"Ger, I'm stuffed!" Jeffrey called out. "I couldn't handle one more bite."

There was some rustling from the kitchen, then Geri returned with a tapered candle in her hand. She stuck it in the half loaf of bread and lit the wick. "Not asking you to eat more, just to make your birthday wish."

His eyes lost that distant look and glistened as he stared at the candle. Cyd thought how he seemed almost boyish, as though he were embarrassed at the attention.

"Shall we sing?" Geri asked, placing her hand on Cyd's shoulder.

"Oh, no..." Jeffrey raised his hands as though to stop them.

"Oh, yes, he wants us to!" Cyd put down her fork and cleared her throat. "Happy birthday to you..."

Babette barked, they sang, and the commotion took on a party atmosphere.

When they finished, Geri fisted her hands on her ample hips. "Time to make a wish. And remember, life's about choices."

He leaned toward the candle and paused. And in the briefest of moments, he looked up at Cyd with such a look of yearning, her breath caught in her throat.

He blew out the flame.

"What'd you wish for?" Cyd blurted.

"Now, sweetie girl, if he tells, it won't come true." Geri picked up a few plates and headed for the kitchen. Babette followed, tail wagging.

A comfortable silence fell between Cyd and Jeffrey as they listened to Geri baby-talking the dog in the other room. It felt good sitting quietly with him, almost as though they'd been doing this for years. Suddenly she realized they'd abandoned their push-and-pull chess game.

Or maybe she'd been the only one playing it.

"What do you normally do on your birthday?" Cyd finally asked.

"Nothing."

"Nothing?"

"Is there an echo?" he teased.

She gave a little shrug. "Sorry. Just seems...funny not to celebrate a birthday."

"Well, some of the foster families did things like bake a cake, but when you know you're just passing through, not one of the family, it can feel odd as a kid to celebrate the day of your birth."

Foster families. More than one. She had a knack for asking whatever question came to mind, but this time she held back. Something told her to not pry into his childhood. "And later? Didn't you do special things as an adult?"

He studied her for a moment. "I'm always one to take a friend out for a martini, no matter what the occasion."

"Wasn't there ever..." She licked the bottom of her lip, hesitating. Oh hell, she might as well ask. "A former Mrs. Bradshaw? Or someone..." *Who's Ashley?* "You know, someone special who fussed over things like your birthday."

"A former Mrs.—" Jeffrey laughed. "No, missed that by a hairsbreadth, I'm glad to say. But before we went our separate ways, yes, she was big on planning things like birthday parties even though I told her repeatedly it wasn't my style." He crossed his arms over his chest. "I'm just not a party kinda guy. Especially when they're for me."

A few days ago, she would have thought just the opposite. Seeing Jeffrey that first time in the Alpine Airport, all full of himself in his fancy suit, she would have pegged him as the kind of man who demanded the limelight. But realizing how he grew up, and hearing his not liking fusses made over him, it appeared he was a bit of a loner.

Not unlike herself.

And just a few days ago she recalled his voice being

edgy, demanding, and she'd blamed it on his city slicker mentality.

She'd been wrong there, too. Listening to him now, his voice was mellow. Gentle. Reminded her of her dad.

Funny...both of them Libras, too.

She looked outside the window, wishing she could see the fox again. It had been fun earlier thinking about her dad, how he loved animals. She'd almost forgotten that side of him. *He would have loved living here, being close to the animals, the land...*

The land...

She shifted in her seat, feeling a ripple of anxiousness. While at the White Palace yesterday, Jeffrey had said things about the land, too. How he wanted to share this world's magic with millions of TV viewers.

She imagined seeing the Alaskan country on a screen, stories about the land, the people. But the images crowded in on her, overwhelming her, and suddenly she couldn't differentiate between that screen and the movie theater growing up...

"Weather's let up," Jeffrey said cautiously.

Cyd stood abruptly and began stacking plates, knowing what he was going to say next.

"I need to—"

"I know," she snapped. Avoiding his eyes, she loaded her arms with plates, mugs, glasses and headed to the kitchen.

JEFFREY WASN'T SURE if he loved or hated snowmobiles.

In the last few days, he'd experienced more on this

particular one than he had on anything, in any other part of his life. He'd laughed, fought, and made wild, passionate love on this snowmobile.

And then today he'd experienced yet another chilly, go-to-hell ride on it.

As Cyd cut the engine, Jeffrey slid off and marched through the newly fallen snow toward the Mush Lodge, pondering if he should just stay here, sleep on a cot, and forget the carting back and forth to Geri's. Stomping up the stairs, he thought how just a few hours ago, he'd been waking up naked with Cyd, spooning her, even wondering if what he felt for her was love...

And now he was damn eager to just get her moody self out of his life.

He shoved open the heavy wooden door, greeted with the scents of apple pie and coffee. He paused, taking time to kick the snow off his boots, thinking how ever since the end of breakfast—when he'd quite reasonably brought up his need to revisit the lodge—Cyd, the one-woman weather system, had gone from balmy to blustery.

Jeffrey straightened, headed toward the bar, catching an old Stones tune. Jagger—his voice arrogant and yearning—wailing about wild horses not dragging him away. Jeffrey should be so lucky. A team of wild horses would be a hell of a lot better than relying on Cyd's mercurial taxi service.

Catching Charlie's eye, Jeffrey jabbed his thumb toward the radiophone room. Charlie nodded.

As Jeffrey strode toward the room, he realized something was different in here. Women. Not that he hadn't seen any in here before, but there were more. Almost forty percent, he'd guess. There was a time when he'd scout out such a situation and take his pick. Back when his streetwise ways had sharpened his instincts to the hunt and his conscience didn't overrule his primal nature.

As he sidled around the end of the bar, he nearly ran into a slim, thirtyish woman wearing a long brown dress with bright-flowered embroidery on the top. Her black hair hung thick and shiny to her waist.

"Howdy," she said, grinning expectantly.

"Howdy," he murmured, wondering if they'd met before. She was acting as though they did.

When another woman waved to him, he decided maybe these were people who'd listened to his previous calls, so they felt they knew him. Nothing like being a local celebrity.

When he reached the end of the bar, Jeffrey halted and gestured Charlie over.

"Special martini?" Charlie asked, tossing a blue-and-white checkered dishrag over his shoulder.

"Excellent. I'll need a double. You know, after I return to L.A., I promise to wire you the money to pay my tab—"

Charlie laid a reassuring hand on Jeffrey's arm. "No sweat, brother. I know you're good on your word." He chuckled. "And if you aren't, I know where you work, who you work with..."

"Speaking of which..." Jeffrey glanced around the bar, amazed that almost all eyes were on him. Didn't these people have *any* other sort of entertainment than his next call?

He looked back at Charlie. "Does everyone have to overhear my calls?"

Charlie nodded. "I'll ask the operator for privacy, then you just proceed as usual." He headed toward the radio room and Jeffrey followed.

CYD SAUNTERED INTO THE LODGE and halted. What the hell was with this place?

"Hey, Cyd!" called out Ellie, waving. She sat perched on a stool next to her husband, Don. Ellie and Don lived in a cabin a few miles away, and Cyd had visited several times. Community gatherings, mostly. Ellie made pottery and usually wore jeans and shirts smeared with clay. Today, she wore a butter yellow dress with ruffles.

Cyd fought the urge to groan. *Ruffles?* At least she has enough sense to wear boots, Cyd huffed to herself as she strode to the bar.

On her way, she caught an eyeful of Nan and her teenage daughter Sophie sitting at a nearby table. Was that a skirt Nan was wearing? And was Sophie trussed up in a dress?

Cyd flopped down on a stool and frowned at Charlie.

"How ya doin', Cyd?"

"Fine," she muttered. She looked down the bar and saw Judy, laughing and talking with Jerry. Cyd started to smile, wave hi, when she caught Judy's attire. Cyd frowned, dropped her hand. Another damn frilly dress.

"You having a dance here or something?" Cyd asked, looking back at Charlie.

"No." He wiped something off the bar. "What can I get you, hon?"

"Usual."

He gave her a look, then set a shot glass in front of her. "Having a bad day?"

"No." She forced a smile. "Everything's peachy."

"You never say 'peachy' unless you're having a bad day."

"Why are all the women dressed up?" she blurted, making a mental note to never say "peachy" again for the rest of her life.

"Not sure. When they first started coming in, I thought Jordan was back, throwing himself a birthday bash. Remember that kegger he threw a few years ago?" Charlie emitted a low whistle. "Lasted three days straight. That Jordan, he knows how to show people a good time."

But Cyd had stopped listening. "What do you mean...birthday bash?"

Charlie set the bottle back under the bar. "Today's Jordan's birthday, but he's down in L.A., so that blows my theory on why the ladies are gussied up."

"Today's Jordan's birthday?" Something caught in her chest. Jordan had once mentioned he was adopted. Jeffrey grew up in foster homes.

"October 16," Charlie continued. "I'll never forget it because when he had that kegger, I ordered all the alcohol and food. Must have written that date a hundred times.''

''So today he'd be turning—'' she thought back to a discussion she and Jordan had had earlier this last year when his age came up ''—thirty-five.''

''Sounds about right. May made some of her apple pie—want a slice?''

Cyd shook her head, lost in her thoughts. Jordan and Jeffrey... She tossed back the whiskey, welcoming its sting. Two guys didn't look alike, talk alike, share the same birthday. Hell, come to think of it, they even had those same oversize ears.

She knocked her glass on the bar, signaling Charlie she was ready for another.

He returned and pulled out the bottle, eyeing her. ''I don't mind serving you, hon, but when you seem overly worked up...'' He let the rest of his sentence hang.

She rolled her eyes. ''You know, that was six years ago.''

''Five.''

''Long enough to forget.''

''Things like that I forgive, but never forget. I'm a businessman.''

''Like Jordan.''

Charlie nodded.

Cyd had to admit, Jordan was a smart guy. If she'd applied some of his ''customer relations'' advice these last few days, maybe she wouldn't have crossed wires with Jeffrey so often. Like this morning. Everything was going so well...and then she'd gotten worked up when Jeffrey wanted to make another call from the lodge. It was an automatic reaction because in her heart, she knew he wasn't her enemy.

And she wasn't so obtuse to not comprehend that he truly did bring opportunities for people up here.

But something inside her still felt raw, broken up. A foreboding that life would never be the same. *Can't think about that now.*

Instead she'd take a moment to reassure Charlie she was okay, not "worked up."

She flashed back on one of the customer relations golden rules Jordan used to repeat. *Use "let's" in confrontational discussions because it defuses "us vs. them" and lets the person know you seek a common understanding.*

Straightening, she flashed her most charming smile at Charlie. "Let's..." Let's what? She should have thought this through a little better. "Let's let bygones be bygones," she finally said. "And...let's never let what happened happen again." Plenty of let's there, even a few extra ones for good measure. And she hadn't said the word "peachy." All in all, not bad.

With an amused shake of his head, Charlie murmured, "Cyd, hon, you're a handful, but a damn charming one." He refilled her glass.

JEFFREY EXITED THE RADIO ROOM and headed down the bar, smiling at the sea of faces that turned to him. Had to be that speech he'd made yesterday. People were accepting him. This boded well for the series—as long as Jordan sold it, of course.

He sat down next to Cyd, who looked strangely re-

flective. Maybe she was rethinking her earlier mood.
Maybe she'd be in a better mood.

Maybe he should get out of the business of trying to
figure her out.

"What's a platinum party?" one of the guys asked
from down the bar.

Charlie, who had just set down Jeffrey's drink, exchanged a look with Jeffrey.

"Thought the operator set it up for privacy."

"Not sure what happened, brother. Maybe request-
ing privacy silences only one side?"

A voice down the bar piped up. "Yeah, silences only
the radio side, which stops people from hearing what
the *other* party says."

"Great," Jeffrey said, scratching his beard. "Everyone still heard me."

"Looks like that's how it works." Charlie shrugged.
"Tried to help."

Jeffrey released a sigh. "It's okay, Charlie. You did
the best you could." Long ago, Jeffrey had learned not
to fight the limits of technology. He glanced down the
bar, realizing the man was waiting for an answer to his
question. He hadn't been able to connect with Jordan,
again, so Jeffrey had "pretended" to be himself and
chatted briefly with his secretary Bonnie, who'd reminded him he, well Jordan, was attending a platinum
party that evening.

"A platinum party is...a celebration party," Jeffrey
answered.

"Big-city term," somebody muttered.

"Maybe it's an anniversary party," a woman piped up. "Like a silver wedding anniversary party."

Charlie, washing glasses, looked up at the woman. "Hell, it's probably Jordan's birthday party down there in L.A.!"

Jeffrey paused, assimilating the words. *Jordan. Birthday party.*

"Today's Jordan's birthday?" someone asked.

Charlie nodded. "Poor guy, stuck in L.A. We'll have to make it up to him when he gets back."

Jeffrey turned his head to Cyd, who had an odd glimmer in her eye.

"How old did you turn today?" she asked.

He was vaguely aware she was being civil again, but that paled in comparison to Jordan having a birthday, *today.* "Thirty-five."

She blew out a gust of air. "That cinches it, for sure. Jordan turned thirty-five today, too."

Understanding hit him fully. "He's..." What were the odds of two siblings finding each other in a remote part of the world? One in a million? Two million? But such things happened, one read such stories every day in the paper.

Cyd just stared at him, her eyes big and dark.

"He's my brother," Jeffrey murmured.

He looked into the mirror behind the bar, flashing back to all those years ago when he'd find refuge in a bar where he'd while away hours reading, listening to music, thinking how a barroom was the only home he'd ever really known. How he'd never be like other people and belong to a home, be part of a family.

I have a brother. "Was...is...Jordan married?"

"No."

"Does he have...children?" Jeffrey felt desperate to know if there were others. Nieces, nephews. *Family.*

"No. Not that he's told me, but I think everyone would know if he did."

Right. No real privacy up here. People would know if there were children.

I have a brother.

"Mr. Bradshaw?"

Cyd shifted and saw Sally Nichols standing behind Jeffrey. Cyd frowned. *Another* dress? Except Sally had gone all out and worn something that looked more like a fancy nightie than a dress, for God's sake. All gauzy and white and if Cyd squinted a little, it was damn near see-through.

"Yes?" Jeffrey answered, turning.

Charlie, winding his way down the bar, smiled at her as he refilled Jeffrey's glass.

"Sally," Cyd blurted, "since when did you start wearing nightgowns in public?"

"It's not a nightgown," Sally huffed. "It's a *dress.*"

"Okay." Cyd gave Sally a cool once-over. "Since when you did you start sleeping in your dresses?"

A baritone voice chortled. "Somebody protect the mirror and chairs!"

Loud laughter.

Cyd glared down the bar. "Shut up." She grabbed Jeffrey's drink and downed it, ignoring Charlie's warning look.

Sally turned her attention back to Jeffrey. "Mr. Bradshaw," she began again, her voice light and breathy. "I'd like to introduce myself. Sally Nichols." She extended her hand.

They shook.

Cyd glared at their clasped hands, wondering if she should toss some ice water on Sally.

"I'd like to apply for a position as an extra." Sally heaved in a breath that made her breasts strain so tight against the bodice, Cyd swore those puppies were going to break loose any second.

She swerved her glare to Jeffrey. "How long you gonna hold hands?"

Jeffrey looked down, then edged his hand out of Sally's. "Cyd, it was only a handshake."

"Handshakes last a few seconds. Longer, it's something else. And while we're on the subject, who the hell's Ashley?"

The bar grew eerily quiet, except for the mournful strains of Jagger singing goodbye to Ruby Tuesday.

"Ashley?" Jeffrey said, a perplexed look on his face. "What does she have to do with this?"

"That's what I'd like to know!" She was doing it again. Sounding shrill, feeling irrational as hell. Feelings—jealousy, insecurity, white-hot fury—were all balled up inside of her and she felt like smashing something.

She slid off her stool, her feet hitting the floor with a solid thud. She stomped away a few feet, furious at herself for losing it, furious at Jeffrey, furious at anything that moved or breathed.

One of the guys guffawed, muttering something about her not wearing a dress.

That sonofa...like *she* couldn't compete with the other women!

Cyd spun around and glared at everyone, their faces blurry through the emotion filling her eyes. All those dresses...all those women showing off to Jeffrey...

Cyd clomped back to the bar and picked up a chair.

Gasps.

Someone hooted.

"Cyd!" Charlie yelled.

She felt an arm on hers. She shot a glance to the side and saw her aunt, her arms filled with some cans—convenience goods Charlie kept stocked for purchase. Worse, Cyd saw Geri's pitying look, which made Cyd feel stupid and ridiculous for losing it like this.

She set down the chair. Anger and hurt swept all the way from her toes, forcing the breath out of her body. "I want all of you—" her voice was shaking; she cleared it "—to can the chair and mirror jokes."

Silence.

She picked up the chair again.

"Okay, Cyd, jeez!" someone yelled.

"I mean it!" she barked. "Just 'cause I can whoop any guy's ass in here at any game doesn't mean I'm not—" she glanced at Sally's dress, her insides caving in "—soft, too," she whispered.

The room was so quiet, the light thump of the chair settling back on to the floor sounded thunderous.

Cyd turned, stormed to the door and exited.

11

GERI PULLED HER SNOWMOBILE up in front of her cabin and killed the engine. Jeffrey slid off the seat from behind her, damn grateful to see Cyd's machine parked near the porch. Good. She was here.

Almost an hour ago at the Mush Lodge, he and Geri had watched Cyd speed away on the snowmobile. Geri had told Jeffrey Cyd wouldn't do anything foolish, but he'd still worried. The lady had a wildly impulsive side.

But, fortunately, she'd curbed it and driven straight home.

"I'll grab the supplies," he said, gathering several plastic bags.

"Thanks, Jeff." Geri said, reaching for the gas cap. "I'll be right in after I check the fuel level."

He trudged toward the cabin, eyeing the darkening sky. Another storm front was expected this afternoon. Charlie had warned them about it as they left the lodge, said it was expected to last one day, most likely two. White-out conditions.

Which meant Jeffrey wouldn't be traveling back and forth to the lodge for a while. Which forced him to be hands off, to trust Jordan would do a good job. If life was about lessons, Jeffrey decided this had to be his—

to back off from being such a hands-on manager. His best pal Rob had his act together, and from what Jeffrey had seen of True North Airlines, so did Jordan.

Interesting how he and his brother both excelled in business—had to be in the genes.

Besides, right now something else was foremost on Jeffrey's mind. *Cyd.* He couldn't shake the image of her back at the lodge, facing a crowd of people with that chair in her hands, a look of hurt and devastation on her face.

He pushed open the door and went in.

The cabin was warm, touched with lingering scents of bacon and coffee from breakfast. Babette greeted him, her tail wagging.

No Cyd.

He carried the groceries into the kitchen.

No Cyd.

He set the bag down and headed back to the living room just as Geri came in. "Sweetie girl, we're home," she called out. She started to head to the kitchen.

"She's not in there," said Jeffrey.

"Maybe she's lying down, taking a nap," Geri turned, headed down the hallway.

Cyd never took naps, not from what Jeffrey had seen. She had enough energy for two people. Sometimes three. He glanced out the window again, reassuring himself that that was indeed Cyd's snowmobile parked outside. Well, Harry's snowmobile. Jeffrey recalled the engraved words on the bar top.

Harry loves Cyd.

He wondered if Harry still did.

Geri walked back into the room. "She's not in the bedroom or bathroom."

They looked in all the rooms.

Except for...

"I'll go downstairs," Jeffrey said, "check the basement."

Moments later, he headed down the wooden stairs into the dimly lit room. There, on a stool next to the oil-stove sat Cyd, hunched over, pointing a flashlight at something she held. As he moved closer, he recognized it as the family photo from upstairs.

She didn't look up.

"Cyd?" he said softly.

She raised her head.

The single overhead bulb cast a feeble light in the room. But even in the hazy glow, he saw the sadness etched in her face. A painful tightening stretched around his heart.

"You okay?"

She nodded, then snapped off the flashlight and set it aside.

He didn't like looming over her. Looking around, he spied a large wooden bucket that he grabbed and turned upside down in front of her. Sitting on it, he met her at eye level.

Closer, he saw her swollen eyes. She'd been crying. And her hair, which always had a mind of its own, looked as though it had gone on strike. It stuck out in every conceivable direction, as though she'd been dragging her fingers through it.

This was a woman who always needed a secret place

to let down her guard, whether it be that frozen meadow they'd visited yesterday or the dark basement today. Must have been hell on her to have exposed her vulnerability in front of the gang at the lodge. They were accustomed to tough, rowdy Cyd, not the emotional, *soft* woman who sat before him now.

"Want to talk?" he asked gently.

Her mouth twisted. "Haven't I said enough today?"

"Well, you certainly know how to wow a room."

"You mean *stun* a room."

"That, too."

Her brows pulled together in a question. "You must think I'm crazy."

"The thought's crossed my mind," he teased.

"Stuck in Katimuk with a crazy woman."

"Actually, we're both stuck in a cabin in Katimuk for the next forty-eight hours. Charlie says the brunt of the storm's finally arrived."

"How are you going to get to your radio calls? You must feel anxious, your business—"

"Right now, I'm more anxious about your well-being."

"I can take care of myself," she whispered.

"I think everyone in Katimuk knows that." He pulled off his glove and laid his hand on hers. "Let me help take care of you, too, Cyd."

Cyd swallowed hard, fighting to contain the emotion churning within her. She felt exposed, frightened, but underneath all that, grateful. No guy had ever made an offer to take care of her. Probably because he didn't dare. Most folks knew too well how she treated offers of help. She'd ignore them or make a sarcastic remark.

But right now she was too exhausted to get her hackles up. Plus, for the first time, she didn't want to handle everything by herself. She was ready to let someone in.

Someone like Jeffrey.

They sat in the quiet, the only sounds an occasional creak or pop from the oilstove.

She liked how a slant of hazy light fell across his face. She'd never really noticed before the set of his mouth, almost grim when he was serious. Or the way his brow furrowed with thought.

"Cyd," he said, breaking the silence. "I'd like to talk about your family."

She tightened her grip on the photo. "Why?"

"Because...I want you to think about something," he continued, his voice deep with concern. "You've thought before that my business plans might destroy your world. I hope you feel differently now. What I'd like you to think about is...maybe what you're afraid of is not the change I'd bring, but the change that's already taking place...has been taking place for a long time..."

"What change?" she croaked. The sensations she'd experienced in the bar—feeling raw, broken up—returned with a vengeance. A dark foreboding, that life would never be the same, rippled through her.

"You're your father's legacy, not his replacement. You can spread your wings, Cyd, be whatever you want to be. An engineer, maybe."

Another thing Geri had told Jeffrey. Those two

seemed to chat a lot when Cyd wasn't around. She cleared her throat. "I could never leave my family. They need me."

"On the ride home, Geri mentioned your seventeen-year-old brother is an adventure guide. And that your mother's doing well as a bookkeeper for several businesses."

"I can't leave."

"Why?"

"I might return and..."

Jeffrey looked intently at her. "And?"

"It'll all be gone," she said in a strangled voice. Memories came flooding back, rushing out in words. "The way the theater disappeared. Vanished into thin air. Replaced by a parking lot." She'd never told anyone about her visit to Seattle, right before her dad died, when her mom had insisted Cyd go away for a few days and visit her best girlfriend back home. While there, Cyd had gone to see the old theater, and was horrified to discover it was totally and completely gone. As though it had never existed.

And in her fourteen-year-old mind, she'd made a link between the building and her dying father. He'd soon be gone, too. As though he never existed. And she'd sworn to herself that would never happen. Not as long as she took his place, kept the family together exactly as he had.

Jeffrey touched Cyd's arm, bringing her back to the present. "If you let go of your role as family caretaker, your family won't disappear."

Letting go. She felt herself go cold, as though her life

blood was draining from her body. For a sickening moment, she thought she'd be ill. "I don't want to talk anymore," she said between clenched teeth.

He nodded solemnly. "Let's go upstairs."

And as they headed up the stairs, Cyd clutched the picture tightly to her chest.

MINUTES LATER, CYD WAS rehanging the photo on the wall when Geri called out from her bedroom, "Cyd, sweetie, could you come back here for a minute?"

Cyd headed down the hallway, and halted when she stepped into her aunt's room.

There, on the bed, lay a long, pink dress.

Not just pink, but a frothy, light pink. Like alpenglow, the rosy color that reflected off mountains at sunset. "When did you get this?" whispered Cyd, her insides melting at the sight.

"It's May's."

"*Charlie's* May? Why do you have it?"

Geri, suddenly absorbed with checking something on the dress, mumbled she was helping May.

"Helping May? How?" Cyd thought a moment. "Oh, please don't tell me she wants to be an extra, too."

"Uh, no, she's...giving it to her niece."

"What niece?"

Geri mumbled something about a niece visiting any day. "So I need to hem it," Geri finished.

Cyd stared at her aunt, whose cheeks were almost as pink as the dress. Calm, collected Geri, flustered? "Can't May hem it?"

"She doesn't sew."

"Neither do you!"

Geri brushed something off the dress, avoiding Cyd's eyes. "Took it up this last year. It's a new hobby."

Cyd glanced around the bedroom, whose décor was "early stack." Stacks of clothes over a chair. Stacks of books on the floor, the dresser. And when one looked under the stacks, they found functional furniture and an occasional piece of equipment like a fishing rod or a hammer.

Hardly the room of a woman who recently took up sewing as a hobby.

But when Cyd looked back at her aunt, the thoughts flew out of her head as she stared again at the piece of pink confection her aunt was holding up. When Geri gave it a little shake, the chiffon made a gentle swishing sound.

Cyd was mesmerized.

"I need you to try it on," Geri said.

Cyd's breath caught in her throat. "Me?"

"I can't hem it without it being on a model."

"I'm no model."

"Toss your clothes on the chair, on top of the other clothes," Geri said, ignoring Cyd's comment.

"Shouldn't the niece model it when she gets here?"

"Oh. Well, it's actually a *gift* for May's niece. Can't model a gift and be surprised. Hell, no. Sooner I get this hemmed, sooner May can wrap it, have it ready. I'm tired of talking. Take off your clothes and let's get this on you."

JEFFREY SAT IN FRONT of the wood-burning stove, Babette at his feet. He stared at the photo on the wall, looking at the fourteen-year-old girl who stood in the forefront. He couldn't see her too clearly sitting this far away, but recalled the dress, the long styled hair and of course, those big chocolate brown eyes.

He wondered how that girl would have evolved if the theater had survived, if her family hadn't moved to the North. If she hadn't adopted that tough shell to protect her vulnerability. But most of all, he wondered if Cyd had understood what he was saying downstairs. He wanted what was best for her, and he hoped she'd understand that at the very least.

A blur of movement distracted him.

He looked over. His mouth dropped open.

There stood Cyd, looking like something that stepped out of *Vogue* magazine. She was a vision in pink, lovelier than anything he'd ever seen. Her hair was brushed and neatly parted, one side tucked flirtatiously behind one ear. She wore a pair of freshwater pearl earrings that shimmered in the light.

But the dress...oh the dress.

"What?" he asked, wrestling with the dramatic transformation. "Why?"

Geri, hovering behind Cyd, said, "I needed Cyd to model it for me. I'm going to hem it."

"Oh..." Jeffrey's gaze traveled over Cyd.

The top fitted her snugly, the round neckline offering a teasing hint of cleavage. The dress cinched at her waist, then flared into a cloud of chiffon that floated down to her bare feet.

The last part added a touch of titillation to the image. A stunningly feminine dress and no shoes. Only a stone-cold male wouldn't fantasize that maybe, just as she didn't wear shoes, she wore nothing else under that frilly number. Sin dipped in heaven.

"Cyd," he said, realizing he'd been staring at her in silence. "You look absolutely beautiful."

Geri beamed.

"Prettier than Sally Nichols?" Cyd blurted.

Jeffrey wanted to laugh at the burst of Cydism, but knew he'd forever regret this moment if he did. "More beautiful than Sally."

"And Ashley?"

He was waiting for this name to pop up again. Time to nip it. "Ashley is a co-worker, nothing more. In fact, at work I call her the Iron Maiden. Hardly a term of endearment."

Cyd looked relieved. Sort of.

"For the record," he continued, "let me state unequivocally that you look more beautiful than any woman I've ever laid my eyes on."

You're the girl in the photo, all grown up.

Amazing. Cyd was turning crimson. He'd embarrassed her with his compliments. He loved seeing this side of her. A little timid, blushing, nervous. And oh so very soft. A woman powerful in her mystique.

"My turn," he said.

Cyd blinked. "What?"

"What's with 'Harry loves Cyd'?" He wouldn't normally ask such a question with a third party present, but these Alaskan ways were wearing off on him. Nothing was really private.

Cyd's mouth formed a little O. "That was a long time ago. When I wore my heart on my sleeve."

"You don't do that anymore?"

Cyd stared at Jeffrey so long, he wondered if she'd heard his question.

Geri suddenly stepped around Cyd. "I, uh, left my thread at Calvin's."

Cyd looked surprised. "What are you talking about?"

Geri walked across the room to where the coats hung and grabbed her parka. "Left the thread there when I dropped off the package of moose meat yesterday."

"You dropped off moose meat and *thread?*" asked Cyd.

Her aunt stepped into her boots while craning her neck to look out the window. "Would ya look at the snow starting to fall. Yes indeed, this is going to be the worst of the storm." She turned and lumbered to the door. "Probably best if I stay at Calvin's. Don't want to risk driving back in bad weather."

Cyd fisted her hands on her hips. "He only lives a hundred yards away—"

"Remember to feed Babette. Plenty of food in the kitchen." Geri stuck her beaver cap on her head and opened the door. Cold air swept into the room.

"What's going on between you and Calvin?" Cyd blurted, shivering a little. She wrapped her arms around herself.

Geri smiled over her shoulder. "Why, sweetie girl,

the same thing that's going on between you and Jeffrey."

The door shut behind her with a solid thunk.

After a pause, Jeffrey turned back to Cyd, whose mouth had dropped open. He didn't think he'd ever seen Cyd struck speechless before.

"Don't tell me you hadn't guessed that already," he said.

She slid a look at him. "Calvin has lived next door long as I can remember. And he's sixty-two!"

"You think love ends at a certain age?"

"No, but..." She shivered again.

"You're cold," Jeffrey said, rising to his feet. "Come over here in front of the fire."

"I should take off this dress."

"Oh, don't worry," he said, his voice growing low, husky. "We will."

Cyd shivered again, but this time it had nothing to do with the cold. She looked Jeffrey over, appreciating his rugged masculinity as though this were the first time she'd ever set eyes on him. He stood tall, his body the kind of V shape other men *wished* they had. The dark green shirt made those sexy hazel eyes stand out. And the way he filled a pair of jeans was downright illegal.

But the best part was the way he looked at her. He was a man who knew his way around words, but what he said with that look in his eyes made her knees shake.

He waggled his fingers, urging her to him.

She floated to him and he scooped her into his arms,

his embrace warm and comforting and electrifying. She stood on tiptoe and closed her eyes, puckering her lips for one mind-melding, toe-curling kiss.

Nothing.

She opened her eyes. He'd pulled his head back, his lips just out of reach.

"This time we take it slow," he whispered.

She blinked. *Yeah, right.* She dove for his lips.

And hit air.

"Cyd," he murmured, gripping her arms. "I love your passion. God, I love it. But, this time, let's savor each other. Like a fine wine."

"I drink whiskey."

"Like a fine whiskey, then."

Jeffrey paused, feeling the tension in her body under his fingers. When she relaxed a little, he slid his hands up her arms and cradled her face, enjoying her tender, sweet look...while knowing damn well she could be anything but. He loved that. What other woman could fly a Cessna in a snow squall without breaking a sweat, and also dress up like a piece of mouthwatering candy?

Cyd. They broke the mold when they made her.

"Dance with me," he murmured, pulling her close. He held one of her hands while pressing his palm against the small of her back.

"I'm not—" she hesitated "—real good at dancing."

"Humor the birthday boy." He stepped one way, then the other. "One, two. One, two," he said, the distant clicking of a clock helping him mark time.

After a few misses, she fell into step with him. "There's no music," she whispered.

"Sing whatever it was that you sang in the shower yesterday."

She paused, then began humming the old Springsteen tune, the melancholy one about a woman's secret garden. Jeffrey danced them slowly over to the light switch. He flipped it, dousing the room in shadow except for the flickering light from the wood-burning stove.

He slid both arms around her, cuddling her close. Firelight gleamed golden in her eyes. He was entranced by her voice, low and honeyed, and he swore the tune resonated throughout her entire body.

Cyd wasn't sure how long they danced while she hummed and softly sang, but suddenly she realized they'd stopped and were simply standing, holding each other. She looked up into Jeffrey's face, suppressing a shudder as the heat of his hand slid to her nape.

He dipped his head.

She parted her lips.

But his mouth slid past hers as his lips brushed her forehead, temples, hair with a gentle rain of kisses. Bending lower, he couched a kiss at the vulnerable hollow of her throat that sent electrical pulses skittering across her skin. Her head fell back and a low, needy moan escaped her lips.

One arm cushioning her, his lips played wicked games...nibbling and licking and kissing her neck, the sensitive spot behind an ear, the exposed skin above her breasts. Her pants grew hungrier when, with his free hand, he traced a sizzling path along her collarbone...back and forth...

"Lower," she whispered.

"What, honey? Slower?"

He gently pulled her back up so she faced him. She stood, dazed, making a small wheezing sound as she struggled to breathe. This man was going to kill her with this slower stuff...

"I...need you," she said, unable to disguise the lowdown greed in her voice.

He leaned forward, his lips so close she felt his warm breaths on her cheek. Finally, oh dear God finally, his mouth pressed against hers and she almost cried out loud at the brush of his lips, hot and searing like lightning.

Fever rose in her body and she gasped as his tongue probed her mouth. She reciprocated, her tongue exploring his wet cavern. He tasted good, hot and sweet, and she clung to his lips with hers, tangling her tongue with his, aching and wanting...

She heard a distant sound that seemed to go on forever. Foggily she realized Jeffrey was unzipping the back of her dress and she squirmed, just a little, in eager anticipation to be free of any constraints.

The dress loosened.

Inhaling a sharp breath, she leveled him a get-this-off-me-*now* look.

He didn't.

He took his sweet time, inching down the bodice. Just enough to expose her nipples, her arms still pinned by the sleeves.

"Your breasts—" Jeffrey's fingers feathered across her mounds "—are so gorgeous."

Her nipples hardened as he skimmed over her breasts again. His touch was like brushing fire on her skin. When his hand pulled away for a moment, she whimpered in protest, and he returned, circling fire around a distended nipple.

Liquid heat pooled hot between her thighs.

She was on the edge, quivering and aching and...

And then she did the unthinkable.

Her knees collapsed and she would have hit the floor had Jeffrey not caught her in his arms.

He looked down at her, his eyes wide. "Cyd, are you okay?"

Gasping for breaths, she looked up at him beseechingly. "If we go any slower," she rasped, "honest to God I'll dissolve and there'll be nothing to make love to."

"Cyd, oh Cyd." He stifled a throaty laugh as he helped her stand again. "I wanted it to feel good for you, not insufferable."

"Slow is good." She nodded as though that would reinforce what she was saying even if she didn't believe a word of it. "But taking me before I melt is even better."

He grabbed the pelt off the back of a nearby chair and tossed it onto the floor before the fire.

"Turn around," he said.

She did.

He quickly tugged the zipper down the last inch or

so and started to pull the sleeves of the dress down, when Cyd laid her hand on his.

"What is it?" he asked.

"Be careful," she whispered. "My heart...it's on that sleeve."

He paused and kissed her neck. "Honey," he whispered, "I'll be careful with it for the rest of my life."

A thrill zinged through her. *Rest of his life. Our life.* She blinked back emotion as he gently pulled the dress off her shoulders, down her back, all the way down to her feet.

"Step out, honey."

She did. Jeffrey whisked the garment away.

He made a throaty, appreciative sound. "You wore nothing underneath."

"Geri told me the faded cotton undies had to go."

"Three cheers for Geri," he murmured huskily, turning Cyd around to face him again. "Let's lie you down, baby." Holding her hand, he walked her the few steps to the fur.

She lay down, liking the lush feel of the pelt against her nakedness. Liking even better the look on Jeffrey's face as his gaze traveled hungrily over her body. "You have a body made for sex..."

He tugged off his shirt and pants and she took in the sight of his muscled form, her body fiery with the need to feel, taste, experience him again.

And when he stepped toward her, she instinctively held open her arms, welcoming him. He lowered himself and lay on top of her. She closed her arms around him, holding him tight.

Above the stove she saw the outline of the family photo, stray light glinting off the glass, the picture dark.

Like the past, she suddenly thought, it's dark, distant. Always there to remember, but no longer alive. She tightened her hold on Jeffrey, absorbing his warmth, feeling his heart beating against hers.

It was time to welcome her future...

12

"HERE KINDA EARLY, AREN'T YA?" Charlie stood behind the Mush Lodge bar, setting a piece of steaming apple pie on the counter in front of him.

Jeffrey flipped his wrist, checked the time: 7:00 a.m. The storm broke last night, so first thing this morning Cyd drove him to the lodge so she could call Wally and set up flights for Jeffrey before they headed to the Cessna. She recalled there being a commuter hop from Alpine to Anchorage where he could catch, best her memory recalled, a direct flight at eight-thirty from Anchorage to Los Angeles.

Which meant, factoring the time difference, Jeffrey would be landing in L.A. around 1:30 p.m. Pacific time, which was when the board meeting was scheduled to end. That would give Jeffrey a small window of time to connect with Jordan, learn the outcome of the series, and most important, break the news that they're brothers.

"What's my tally?" Jeffrey asked Charlie, who was digging his fork into the pie.

"For what?" Charlie asked.

"For at least eight whiskeys, several bowls of caribou stew, and the best homemade French fries I've ever tasted."

"You shoulda tried May's apple pie, too," Charlie quipped with a wink. "No tally. On the house."

"You can't run a business by giving the product away."

"The way I see it..." He held a forkful of pie midair. "I took care of a friend during a tough time. Pass it along, brother." He shoved the steaming sweetness into his mouth.

A few days ago, Jeffrey would have thought that was the craziest piece of advice he'd ever heard. But now it made more sense than anything else. Probably because it epitomized the people of the North, who had their priorities on a hell of a lot straighter than the rest of the world. First and foremost, you took care of each other.

Jeffrey nodded, "You got it, Charlie."

"And one more thing." Charlie paused, putting down his fork to take a sip of coffee. "Take good care of Cyd."

Jeffrey took in a breath, debating how to answer. "She's not going with me." Truth was, he hadn't asked her. But then, Cyd hadn't mentioned it, either. Over the last few days, every time they started to talk about what was going on between them, they'd tumble into something hot and physical.

The *clump clump* of boots. A scent of vanilla, leftover from this morning's lovemaking in the kitchen.

Jeffrey looked at Cyd, who straddled the bar stool next to him. Her hair was wild and spiky, the eyes as big and brown as ever. But her face was different. Relaxed. *Softer.*

He absently scratched his beard. His face was different, too, thanks to there not being a razor at Geri's. But he was toying with keeping it—as an Alaskan memento—when he got back to L.A. Trimmed, of course.

"Got the flight arrangements all worked out," Cyd said. "You'll arrive in L.A. at one-thirty. Wally's leaving messages at Argonaut for Jordan so he can connect with you before his late-afternoon flight."

"Good." Didn't feel so good, though, leaving Cyd. Even temporarily. "You know, Cyd, I've been thinking—"

"Be right there!" she yelled over her shoulder.

Jeffrey glanced behind him. Harry stood inside the front door, an expectant look on his face.

"Dog team's ready to take us to the plane," Cyd said. "We'd better hustle."

For a moment, they looked into each other's eyes and he thought how he'd miss the husky, rich sound of her voice, her stubborn independence, the way she made the world fresh and new again.

The way she made him feel about himself.

That he belonged somewhere, to someone. Not only did he have a brother, but he had Cyd...and the thought of leaving her balled into a cold ache behind his ribs.

"Come with me," he suddenly said. "Take a vacation in Southern California."

One corner of her mouth twisted in a funny grin. "Do women wear parkas there?"

"Pink ones embroidered with rhinestones."

"Sounds practical."

"Come on," he urged. "Thought you sometimes did things on impulse."

"I do..." but she didn't finish her thought, only looked at him with those dark luminous eyes, a flush staining her cheeks. "Let's go," she whispered. "You have a plane—or two or three—to catch."

FIFTEEN MINUTES LATER, the dog sled team slowed to a stop next to the dirt airstrip, covered with snow. The tinkling of the leaders' bells was drowned by a sudden outburst of barks and whines.

Harry jumped off the runners. After setting the snow anchor, he walked down the line of dogs, tossing treats from a bag. Cyd remained in the sled basket, curled close to Jeffrey.

She'd been frowning at the snowy airstrip ever since it came into view.

No Cessna.

"Where's the plane?" asked Jeffrey, his arms wrapped around her as they'd been the entire ride.

Cyd turned slightly and met his eyes. Because the weather was a near-balmy twenty-six degrees, they hadn't bothered to wear ski masks this morning.

Although she was feeling chillier by the second with the situation.

"Don't know," she admitted.

"What do you mean, 'don't know'? We left it here, tied it down."

She felt the tension in his body. This basket had been like a love nest the short ride from the lodge to here, but now it felt tight, claustrophobic.

Cyd grabbed the edges of the basket, hoisted herself up, and jumped onto the snow, sinking a good foot. She trudged to the landing strip and eyed the deep grooves left by the bush wheels, which didn't tell her why someone had taken the plane.

Or who the hell moved it.

Not that it was uncommon for someone to borrow a vehicle. She'd left the ignition key in the plane, just as she always did, especially in winter. People left doors open, keys in trucks, snowmobiles—means to safety or warmth that had often saved lives. But to "borrow" a Cessna without leaving word as to why, was pushing it.

She heard Jeffrey's huffing as he walked up next to her. "What the hell's going on?" he said tightly.

"Like I said, I don't know."

"Seems near impossible for someone to fly off with a Cessna."

"Anyone with pilot experience knew to turn the key, prime the engine and take off. Never had someone do this, though, without my knowing."

The air was still, pulseless, the silence broken only by the creaking of the dogs' harnesses and their yelps as they snatched food from Harry.

Jeffrey scrubbed a hand across his jaw. "Seems you always know more than you let on."

Cyd gave him a double take. "What's that supposed to mean?"

"I think you know."

"No, I don't." She didn't like the look in his eyes. Reminded her of the Jeffrey she'd first met at the Alpine

Airport. Edgy, arrogant. "Why don't you just get it off your chest and ask?"

"*Ask?* I'll just say it. You have a talent, Cyd, for not giving straight answers when it serves your purpose."

Her pulse beat hot in her throat. "I don't like being called a liar," she whispered, feeling her control slipping.

"Well, I don't like being stuck in Katimuk *twice*," he barked. "Once because of weather, and then because of..."

The tension between them had escalated with frightening intensity. "Because of...?" she prompted, feeling angry and sick all at once.

"You."

She gave her head a disbelieving shake. "You think I'd make a *plane disappear* to sabotage your plans?"

"Yes."

She took an involuntary step backward. "After all we've been through..." She clenched her hands at her sides, afraid to say more.

Jeffrey had never said the words, but she'd believed he loved her. But now, looking at the cold anger in his face and hearing his accusation, she decided she'd been wrong. The realization cut deep, like a knife blade to her heart. Jeffrey didn't love her.

He had been...appreciative of her help. That's what it had been. And there'd been chemistry. Enough to ask her to take a vacation with him.

But love?

No, it hadn't been that. Couldn't have been that.

She turned slightly, blinking back the emotion, determined not to lose it in front of him.

"Can't believe I miscalculated the depth of your need to stop my bringing business here," he continued.

She dashed a hand across her eyes. "Oh, give me a break!" She stomped off a few feet, streams of vapor escaping with her breaths. Turning back to him, she said in a strangled voice, "What do you think I did? Convince someone to remove the plane this morning so you couldn't make it back to L.A. in time to meet Jordan?"

"Something like that."

"When would I have done this foul deed? I've been with you every single moment!"

"Except when you were on the radiophone with Wally. Or you *said* it was Wally—"

"You're crazy—"

"Really?" He moved toward her, his eyes glitter-bright with rage. "Up until a few days ago, you were hell-bent to stop me from getting the series up here. Everybody knew that, or are they crazy, too?"

Jeffrey heard a shuffling sound. He looked over at Harry, who was pacing awkwardly, checking his mobile radiophone while taking surreptitious glances at Cyd and Jeffrey. "I can't believe I'm having this discussion in front of Harry," he said between clenched teeth. But then, he should've learned by now that even in this vast frontier, nothing was private.

Jeffrey looked back at the empty airstrip. He'd never allowed himself to get intimate with a business partner or even an adversary for that matter. And this showdown with Cyd was the reason why. Such involvements blinded one to the business at hand. He'd gotten so caught up in Cyd, in whatever he thought they were, he'd lost sight of staying in control, ensuring things were followed through according to plan.

He'd even shifted his priorities, thinking nothing mattered more than to be with her, live his life with her.

But opening one's heart didn't mean someone had the right to exploit it. He'd let down his guard and this was his payback.

Betrayal.

He clenched his teeth, fighting a sour taste that burned like acid all the way down to his stomach. The little actress had really outdone herself this time. He needed to wrap up this insanity, get back to the lodge, handle the next radio call himself.

Get your priorities back in order, buddy.

He and Cyd stared at each other, like two strangers.

Jeffrey turned abruptly and headed back to the sled. "Harry," he yelled, "take us back to the lodge."

A FEW HOURS LATER, CYD sat in Geri's cabin, staring glumly into the fire. How many times had the flames set the mood for hers and Jeffrey's lovemaking these past few days?

Now it seemed like the remnants of their crash and burn.

On the way back to the lodge from the airstrip, she and Jeffrey hadn't exchanged a single word. She was too furious and hurt to talk. Maybe in the beginning she'd have stooped to a stupid disappearing plane trick, but not after what they'd shared these past two days.

Not after falling in love with the guy.

She didn't know it could hurt so bad, feeling falsely indicted, reviled even, by the very man you'd put your faith in, given your heart to. Harry had broken her heart five years ago, but that was like a splintering. With Jeffrey, her heart had shattered.

The front door creaked open. "Hello, sweetie girl!" called out Geri.

"Hey, Geri."

There was a moment's silence, broken only by the wild *thump thump thump* of Babette's tail making contact with the back of a chair as the dog greeted its master.

Cyd didn't want to turn around, didn't want her aunt to see the pain on her face. But damn if a big pair of boots didn't break Cyd's line of vision with the rug.

"I know what happened," Geri said, standing in front of her.

Cyd released a weighty sigh. *Good. I don't have to explain.*

"Smiley's daughter got sick. He borrowed the plane to rush her to Alaska Regional Hospital in Anchorage."

Cyd looked up. "*Smiley* borrowed the plane?"

"Yeah." Geri scratched Babette's head. "Smiley's wife told Charlie, who told me when I dropped by the lodge."

"I didn't know that when I talked to Wally..." When

Cyd and Jeffrey had returned to the lodge, she'd made a beeline for the radiophone and called Wally with the news of the missing Cessna. She'd also requested a backup plane, ASAP, for Jeffrey.

Jeffrey had stood next to her the entire time, as though she might instigate another evil sabotage.

"So," Geri said, sounding abnormally pleasant. "Sounds as though everything worked out, eh? Charlie said Jeffrey's on his way to L.A."

To L.A., out of my life. "That was the plan." She hated this conversation. What happened, happened. She'd picked up her life and started over before, she could do it again.

But she'd never be the same. She'd eventually let go of the hurt and anger, but what she'd shared with Jeffrey would never completely disappear. In just a few days, he'd become a part of her...a precious memory she'd always keep locked in her heart.

"Take off your parka and boots, Geri," she said, trying to sound lighthearted, "and stay awhile."

Her aunt sighed heavily. "Need to get back on the snowmobile, drive back to the lodge. Forgot to drop off the dress to May when I was there."

Cyd looked up. "You never forget anything." She frowned. "And when did you find time to hem it?"

"This morning."

"That was fast."

Geri shrugged. "Hemming's easy." She groaned and rubbed her shoulder. "But the bursitis isn't."

"Bursitis?"

"Started kicking in this last year." Geri scrunched up

her face, groaning as she rubbed her shoulder. "And here I have to get back on the snowmobile, return that dress to May..."

"I still have Harry's snowmobile." After Harry had carted Cyd and Jeffrey back to the lodge, he'd told her to keep the machine as long as she needed.

"Oh, I hate to impose..."

"Since when?" Cyd teased, wondering why she'd never heard about this bursitis. Or for that matter, why she'd never before seen this Southern belle "really, can you help little ol' me" act before. Maybe hanging out with Calvin was bringing out Geri's girlish side.

Cyd stood, welcoming the opportunity to take care of someone else, to take a reprieve from wallowing in her broken heart. "Take off your parka, relax. I'll take the dress back to the lodge."

CYD STEPPED INTO THE MUSH LODGE, scraping her snow-caked feet on the welcome mat. The soulful sounds of an old Stones tune, "Lady Jane," was playing.

Considering how Cyd felt about love this morning, a preferable Stones song would be "Paint It Black."

"Smiley dropped by," called out Charlie. "Said thanks for the plane. His little girl's fine."

"Great." In the grand scheme of things, the child's well-being was all that really mattered. Two people, a shattered heart, were nothing in comparison. Merely blips on life's radar.

Cyd headed to the bar and set the package on the

counter. "Here's May's dress," she said, forcing herself to sound even, together.

"What dress?"

"The one Geri hemmed."

Charlie flashed her a quizzical look. "Geri sews?"

Cyd shrugged. "She hemmed it for May's niece."

"What niece?" Charlie suddenly perked up. "Oh, *our niece.* Right, Geri said she'd find a way to get you— I mean, the dress—back here..."

Get you back here?

Mick's voice crooned on.

Cyd fingered the twine around the plastic-wrapped package, remembering how only a few hours ago, she'd been sitting in this exact spot when Jeffrey had asked her to go with him to L.A., take a leave from Alaska. And in that glorious moment, she'd felt just like those words Mick was crooning. She'd felt *promised* to Jeffrey. Her heart wrenched at the memory.

"You okay, hon?" Charlie asked, wiping his hands on a dish towel as he glanced toward the radiophone room.

"Fine," she lied.

"Oh, look," Charlie said, his tone oddly stilted. "Judy's waving to you."

Cyd frowned at him, wondering why he suddenly sounded as though he were reading a script. She looked in the direction he was pointing. Sure enough, Judy was standing at the door to the radio room, motioning Cyd over.

"What is it?" Cyd yelled.

"Call for you," Judy yelled back.

"Must be Wally," Cyd murmured, "wondering if I've located the Cessna."

"Oh, I already told him," Charlie said quickly, picking up the package.

She paused. "You talked to Wally?"

But her question went unanswered as Charlie exited to the kitchen, the door swinging shut behind him.

She slid off the stool and headed toward Judy, who said, "It's Wally," before flashing a funny smile and heading past Cyd to the bar.

Cyd paused, wondering if everyone was acting so oddly because they weren't sure how to behave around her. Well, she didn't blame them. In the past few days, she'd expressed a gamut of emotions in this very lodge, everything from anger to hurt to love.

That love had run its course, too. Maybe the sooner Cyd acted like nothing happened, everybody around here would act like nothing happened, too.

She headed into the radiophone room, catching the ever-present scent of coffee that seemed to hover here. Earlier, she and Wally had made arrangements for Jeffrey's backup plane and flights, but they hadn't discussed her upcoming flight schedule. After the recent bout of bad weather, many snowed-in communities would need flights of supplies, food.

She picked up the mike. It sounded like dogs were barking on the other end. Not unusual for a canine or two to run around the Alpine Airport, although this sounded like a bunch of them.

"Wally?"

"Cyd?"

Jeffrey's voice.

She clutched the mike, her stomach plummeting. "Yes?"

"I've got quite a screw up on my hands."

So businesslike, so authoritative. As though nothing had happened. "Somebody steal another plane?" she quipped. Or tried to. Her voice sounded strained, hurt. She pursed her lips, not wanting to reveal anymore emotion.

"I missed...my flight," he answered, his words interspersed with huffing as though he were walking. More barking dogs in the background. "Next flight...gets me into L.A.... at rush hour. It'll be a miracle...if I get home by seven tonight. Which means...I'll miss Jordan altogether. He flies out of L.A. late afternoon."

Jordan. She closed her eyes, realizing every time she saw her boss, she'd see Jeffrey's face. As though she'd be able to forget a single detail as it was.

"Therefore," Jeffrey continued, "I've decided to stay in Alpine...hook up with Jordan. Wally made reservations for me...at the Alpine Inn."

"Makes sense," she said softly. "Put Wally on, will you?" *I can't stay on the phone, pretending nothing happened between us.* Maybe this is how it was with big-city types. Love one day, business as usual the next. Except between he and Cyd, the transition had occurred in a matter of hours.

"No sense my flying home tomorrow, Saturday," Jeffrey continued, "so I'm staying in Alpine. Two nights."

"Lots of time for you and Jordan to catch up." She squeezed shut her eyes. "Hey, put Wally on—"

"Right, lots of time," Jeffrey went on. "Jordan can tell me about the outcome of the board meeting, we can have a reunion."

The dogs had quieted. Jeffrey's voice was coming through loud and clear now.

"Yes, a reunion," she whispered. Something the two of them would never share. Funny, after all these years, she'd finally learned to let go of her past. And almost in the same moment, she'd welcomed her future. One she'd share with Jeffrey. Yet in a bittersweet twist of fate, she was having to let go of that, too.

"Hey," she repeated, opening her eyes. "Put Wally on."

"Can't."

Something touched her shoulder. She turned, gasped, dropped the mike. It clattered to the floor as she stared into those familiar eyes.

"Can't," Jeffrey repeated, lowering his voice although he still held the mobile radiophone to his mouth. A few snowflakes dotted his parka. So that's why he was huffing, she realized. *He was walking from outdoors into the lodge.* She caught the tang of pine, and Jeffrey's achingly familiar masculine scent.

They held each other's gaze for a long moment.

"Cyd," he murmured, setting the phone on the table, his eyes never breaking contact with hers. "I was on the backup plane when Wally radioed that it was Smiley who'd borrowed the plane. I asked him to get hold of Harry—that I needed a ride back to the lodge..."

So it had been Harry's dog team she'd heard barking in the background. And Harry's mobile radiophone Jeffrey had called the lodge on. And now she understood why everyone had been acting so oddly. There'd been a coordinated conspiracy to get Cyd and Jeffrey talking again, on the phone and hopefully in person.

"How'd you like to take engineering classes at the University of California in Los Angeles?" Jeffrey asked suddenly.

"Is *that* what you came back to say?" She gave her head a disbelieving shake. Everybody's efforts to get Cyd and Jeffrey to talk didn't mean squat if the guy just wanted to play all's well. Didn't he realize that this morning's accusations, and his subsequent departure, had gutted her?

"No, there's more. How about living in L.A. part of the year?"

She rolled back her shoulders, her pride roaring back to life. "How about an apology for this morning?"

She thought she heard someone clapping in the other room.

Jeffrey loved how Cyd looked right now. Fiery, strong, ready to take on the world and anything in her way...like him. But he also saw the hurt in her eyes, and ached knowing he was the one who put it there.

"You're right, Cyd. I'm rushing things. What I wanted to say first, and in person, is that I'm sorry. I was a fool jumping to conclusions. But even more I wanted to tell you, face-to-face, how much I love that secret place of yours we visited, how much I love the Great White North, but most of all—" his voice dropped to a low, intense tone "—how much I love you." He paused, and when he spoke again, she thought she detected a tremble in his voice. "Nothing is worth anything without you in my life."

She choked back an astonished laugh. "Aren't you the guy who thought I'd stolen a plane?"

"Yes." Jeffrey moved closer, the nearness of her damn near overpowering his senses. "And now I'm the guy accusing you of stealing my heart, too." He paused, cupping her chin and raising it so she couldn't look away. "I'm sorry for what I said earlier, but to be honest..." A hundred memories crowded his mind, shadowed by the stupidity of his reaction this morning. "I'm terrified I blew it. I love you, Cyd. And I want you to—I mean, I'm asking you to—marry me." His voice lowered to a husky whisper. "Baby, let's take the world by storm."

Cyd stared into those glistening hazel eyes that had captured her from the moment they'd met. The familiar thrill stirred in her and she smiled. "What if we get weathered in?"

A slow grin creased his face, then he wrapped his arms around her and pulled her tight against him. Nuzzling her ear, he whispered hotly, "I think you know exactly what we'd do."

"I do," she said softly, riding a rush of love as she heard the words and thought how it would be to say them again, to Jeffrey, in front of all their friends and family.

Outside, in the bar, people broke out in loud whoops and clapping.

"I think we're being listened to," she whispered.

"That's us, the best entertainment around. But when we're down there, our conversations will be more private."

She pulled back and looked into his eyes. "Down there?"

"What do you think about six months in L.A., six months in Alaska? And if L.A. is too—well, too L.A. for you—there's mountains, desert, beaches nearby."

"What about your job at the studio?"

"I'm thinking of ways to still do it, maybe share it. More important is the life I want to share with you. Starting with a few nights in Alpine..."

Their bodies moved together instinctively and she surrendered to the heady sensation of being in Jeffrey's arms. "I'll fly us there," she murmured, inching her lips toward his.

"Just land in the right town," he teased, his mouth so close, his breath mingled with hers.

"Right town, right guy."

Then she kissed him, her heart soaring higher than any plane could fly.

*   *   *   *   *

Find out what happens to Jeffrey's twin Jordan!
Pick up Barbara Dunlop's book

TOO CLOSE TO CALL

Temptation #940
Available now at your local retailer!

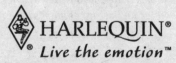

Is your man too good to be true?

Hot, gorgeous AND romantic?
If so, he could be a Harlequin® Blaze™ series cover model!

Our grand-prize winners will receive a trip for two to New York City to shoot the cover of a Blaze novel, and will stay at the luxurious Plaza Hotel.

Plus, they'll receive $500 U.S. spending money!

The runner-up winners will receive $200 U.S. to spend on a romantic dinner for two.

It's easy to enter!

In 100 words or less, tell us what makes your boyfriend or spouse a true romantic and the perfect candidate for the cover of a Blaze novel, and include in your submission two photos of this potential cover model.

All entries must include the written submission of the contest entrant, two photographs of the model candidate and the Official Entry Form and Publicity Release forms completed in full and signed by both the model candidate and the contest entrant. Harlequin, along with the experts at Elite Model Management, will select a winner.

For photo and complete Contest details, please refer to the Official Rules on the next page. All entries will become the property of Harlequin Enterprises Ltd. and are not returnable.

Please visit www.blazecovermodel.com to download a copy of the Official Entry Form and Publicity Release Form or send a request to one of the addresses below.

Please mail your entry to: **Harlequin Blaze Cover Model Search**

In U.S.A.	In Canada
P.O. Box 9069	P.O. Box 637
Buffalo, NY	Fort Erie, ON
14269-9069	L2A 5X3

No purchase necessary. Contest open to Canadian and U.S. residents who are 18 and over.
Void where prohibited. Contest closes September 30, 2003.

HBCVRMODEL1

HARLEQUIN BLAZE COVER MODEL SEARCH CONTEST 3569 OFFICIAL RULES
NO PURCHASE NECESSARY TO ENTER

1. To enter, submit two (2) 4" x 6" photographs of a boyfriend or spouse (who must be 18 years of age or older) taken no later than three (3) months from the time of entry: a close-up, waist up, shirtless photograph; and a fully clothed, full-length photograph, then, tell us, in 100 words or fewer, why he should be a Harlequin Blaze cover model and how he is romantic. Your complete "entry" must include: (i) your essay, (ii) the Official Entry Form and Publicity Release Form printed below completed and signed by you (as "Entrant"), (iii) the photographs (with your hand-written name, address and phone number, and your model's name, address and phone number on the back of each photograph), and (iv) the Publicity Release Form and Photograph Representation Form printed below completed and signed by your model (as "Model"), and should be sent via first-class mail to either: Harlequin Blaze Cover Model Search Contest 3569, P.O. Box 9069, Buffalo, NY, 14269-9069, or Harlequin Blaze Cover Model Search Contest 3569, P.O. Box 637, Fort Erie, Ontario L2A 5X3. All submissions must be in English and be received no later than September 30, 2003. Limit: one entry per person, household or organization. **Purchase or acceptance of a product offer does not improve your chances of winning.** All entry requirements must be strictly adhered to for eligibility and to ensure fairness among entries.

2. Ten (10) Finalist submissions (photographs and essays) will be selected by a panel of judges consisting of members of the Harlequin editorial, marketing and public relations staff, as well as a representative from Elite Model Management (Toronto) Inc., based on the following criteria:

Aptness/Appropriateness of submitted photographs for a Harlequin Blaze cover—70%
Originality of Essay—20%
Sincerity of Essay—10%

In the event of a tie, duplicate finalists will be selected. The photographs submitted by finalists will be posted on the Harlequin website no later than November 15, 2003 (at www.blazecovermodel.com), and viewers may vote, in rank order, on their favorite(s) to assist in the panel of judges' final determination of the Grand Prize and Runner-up winning entries based on the above judging criteria. All decisions of the judges are final.

3. All entries become the property of Harlequin Enterprises Ltd. and none will be returned. Any entry may be used for future promotional purposes. Elite Model Management (Toronto) Inc. and/or its partners, subsidiaries and affiliates operating as "Elite Model Management" will have access to all entries including all personal information, and may contact any Entrant and/or Model in its sole discretion for their own business purposes. Harlequin and Elite Model Management (Toronto) Inc. are separate entities with no legal association or partnership whatsoever having no power to bind or obligate the other or create any expressed or implied obligation or responsibility on behalf of the other, such that Harlequin shall not be responsible in any way for any acts or omissions of Elite Model Management (Toronto) Inc. or its partners, subsidiaries and affiliates in connection with the Contest or otherwise and Elite Model Management shall not be responsible in any way for any acts or omissions of Harlequin or its partners, subsidiaries and affiliates in connection with the contest or otherwise.

4. All Entrants and Models must be residents of the U.S. or Canada, be 18 years of age or older, and have no prior criminal convictions. The contest is not open to any Model that is a professional model and/or actor in any capacity at the time of the entry. Contest void wherever prohibited by law; all applicable laws and regulations apply. Any litigation within the Province of Quebec regarding the conduct or organization of a publicity contest may be submitted to the Régie des alcools, des courses et des jeux for a ruling, and any litigation regarding the awarding of a prize may be submitted to the Régie only for the purpose of helping the parties reach a settlement. Employees and immediate family members of Harlequin Enterprises Ltd., D.L. Blair, Inc., Elite Model Management (Toronto) Inc. and their parents, affiliates, subsidiaries and all other agencies, entities and persons connected with the use, marketing or conduct of this Contest are not eligible to enter. Acceptance of any prize offered constitutes permission to use Entrants' and Models' names, essay submissions, photographs or other likenesses for the purposes of advertising, trade, publication and promotion on behalf of Harlequin Enterprises Ltd., its parent, affiliates, subsidiaries, assigns and other authorized entities involved in the judging and promotion of the contest without further compensation to any Entrant or Model, unless prohibited by law.

5. Finalists will be determined no later than October 30, 2003. Prize Winners will be determined no later than January 31, 2004. Grand Prize Winners (consisting of winning Entrant and Model) will be required to sign and return Affidavit of Eligibility/Release of Liability and Model Release forms within thirty (30) days of notification. Non-compliance with this requirement and within the specified time period will result in disqualification and an alternate will be selected. Any prize notification returned as undeliverable will result in the awarding of the prize to an alternate set of winners. All travelers (or parent/legal guardian of a minor) must execute the Affidavit of Eligibility/Release of Liability prior to ticketing and must possess required travel documents (e.g. valid photo ID) where applicable. Travel dates specified by Sponsor but no later than May 30, 2004.

6. Prizes: One (1) Grand Prize—the opportunity for the Model to appear on the cover of a paperback book from the Harlequin Blaze series, and a 3 day/2 night trip for two (Entrant and Model) to New York, NY for the photo shoot of Model which includes round-trip coach air transportation from the commercial airport nearest the winning Entrant's home to New York, NY, (or, in lieu of air transportation, $100 cash payable to Entrant and Model, if the winning Entrant's home is within 250 miles of New York, NY), hotel accommodations (double occupancy) at the Plaza Hotel and $500 cash spending money payable to Entrant and Model, (approximate prize value: $8,000), and one (1) Runner-up Prize of $200 cash payable to Entrant and Model for a romantic dinner for two (approximate prize value: $200). Prizes are valued in U.S. currency. Prizes consist of only those items listed as part of the prize. No substitution of prize(s) permitted by winners. All prizes are awarded jointly to the Entrant and Model of the winning entries, and are not severable - prizes and obligations may not be assigned or transferred. Any change to the Entrant and/or Model of the winning entries will result in disqualification and an alternate will be selected. Taxes on prize are the sole responsibility of winners. Any and all expenses and/or items not specifically described as part of the prize are the sole responsibility of winners. Harlequin Enterprises Ltd. and D.L. Blair, Inc., their parents, affiliates, and subsidiaries are not responsible for errors in printing of Contest entries and/or game pieces. No responsibility is assumed for lost, stolen, late, illegible, incomplete, inaccurate, non-delivered, postage due or misdirected mail or entries. In the event of printing or other errors which may result in unintended prize values or duplication of prizes, all affected game pieces or entries shall be null and void.

7. Winners will be notified by mail. For winners' list (available after March 31, 2004), send a self-addressed, stamped envelope to: Harlequin Blaze Cover Model Search Contest 3569 Winners, P.O. Box 4200, Blair, NE 68009-4200, or refer to the Harlequin website (at www.blazecovermodel.com).

Contest sponsored by Harlequin Enterprises Ltd., P.O. Box 9042, Buffalo, NY 14269-9042.

HBCVRMODEL2

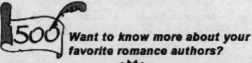

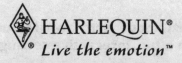

HARLEQUIN®
Temptation®

*Legend has it that
the only thing that can bring down a Quinn
is a woman...*

Now we get to see for ourselves!

The youngest Quinn brothers have grown up.
They're smart, they're sexy...and they're about to be
brought to their knees by their one true love.

Don't miss the last three books in
Kate Hoffmann's dynamic miniseries...

The Mighty Quinns

Watch for:

THE MIGHTY QUINNS: LIAM
(July 2003)

THE MIGHTY QUINNS: BRIAN
(August 2003)

THE MIGHTY QUINNS: SEAN
(September 2003)

Available wherever Harlequin books are sold.

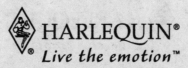

HARLEQUIN®
Live the emotion™

Visit us at www.eHarlequin.com

HTMQ

It's romantic comedy with a kick
(in a pair of strappy pink heels)!

Introducing

"It's chick-lit with the romance and happily-ever-after ending that Harlequin is known for."
—*USA TODAY* bestselling author Millie Criswell, author of *Staying Single*, October 2003

"Even though our heroine may take a few false steps while finding her way, she does it with wit and humor."
—Dorien Kelly, author of *Do-Over*, November 2003

Launching October 2003.
Make sure you pick one up!

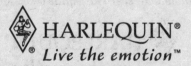